Affairs of the Heart, Volume 2

Kristi Lea

This is a work of fiction. Names, places, events, and characters are the product of the author's imagination or are used fictitiously. Any similarity to real people, places, or events is entirely coincidental.

First Printing, 2016

ISBN: 978-0-9982045-2-9

www.KristiLea.com

About the Author

A voracious reader since before she can remember, Kristi has always been drawn to romance, science fiction, and fantasy, or, preferably all three at once. Now, when she isn't reading her favorite books to herself or to her kids, she is writing her own stories. Kristi, her husband, and their two children live with a pair of cats rescued from the streets of suburban St. Louis.

Visit her online at **www.KristiLea.com**

CHAPTER ONE

Sweat streaked down the back of Kelsie Forrester's halter dress, soaking the ties of her bikini and making the fabric stick to her hot, sunburned skin. She dialed, again, and held her cell phone to one ear, again, and got yet another litany of ringing with no answer. From across the street, an engine gunned and tires shrieked on the shimmering pavement. She danced from foot to foot on the hot white sand as she watched the back of a red pickup truck turn onto Ocean Boulevard towards downtown Palm Beach.

Her favorite flip flops were in that truck. So was her boyfriend. Rather, her ex-boyfriend. And his new girlfriend. Kelsie glared at the receding taillights. She was going to miss those flip flops.

Her cell phone beeped its low-battery warning, again, and the ringing on the other end finally switched over to voicemail. Her mother never seemed to hear the cell phone anymore. Or she lost it. Or left it buried in the bottom of her tote bag for a week until the battery finally ran out. Kelsie's brother Helmut kept wondering if their mother was starting to show early signs of dementia or Alzheimer's. Kelsie thought that their mom simply didn't care about the cell phone. It didn't matter whether the problem was forgetfulness or disdain, though. Today, it looked like Kelsie would be walking three miles back to her mom's house. Barefoot.

She hot-footed it to one of the benches that lined the parking lot and flopped down. She rubbed her scorched soles for a minute before digging through her beach bag hoping to find some long-forgotten socks, or maybe twenty bucks for a cab. Instead, she found sunscreen, her towel, a mini-wallet containing her driver's license and University of St. Thomas ID, seventy-six cents, two hair ties, a fat comb, chapstick, a tattered romance novel, and the torn ticket stub from the beach volleyball tournament she'd come to watch. No footwear. Not even enough change for the bus.

Her two-timing rat bastard of a boyfriend had been playing in the tournament today, and she had spent the rest of her cash buying a prime seat so she could cheer him on. The jerk even won, and had blown her a kiss in between fist pumps and high-fives with the rest of his team. And then, as usual, he left her sitting there all alone in his car for the better part of an hour while he and his buddies did their usual post-game routine: Packing up, changing clothes, laughing and joking and generally having a lot of fun.

This time, he was having more fun than usual. With the new girl who had just joined their co-ed volleyball team a month prior. The same girl that he had joked was as flat-chested and narrow-hipped as a boy, but who had a wicked spike. Volleyball prowess must be far more attractive than the slimeball had ever admitted to.

Kelsie's cell phone warbled its final death knoll and then shut itself down. Not that it would do her any good. If her mom wasn't around, she had no one else to call. Her brother, Helmut, lived in Chicago with his fiancée, and her other brother Rob was off in the Brazilian jungle studying frogs. Her best friend Alice had stayed in Miami for the summer in their shabby off-campus apartment. Most of her other friends from undergrad still lived down in Miami, or else had escaped to parts far and wide to pursue their own graduate degrees. She contemplated the sidewalk, and then her feet, and then the sidewalk again. This was going to hurt.

The young man in the black trousers and fluorescent green restaurant T-shirt, with his short waiter's apron still tied around his waist, slammed his foot into the side of the metal dumpster and let loose with a long diatribe of insults and accusations.

Marquez Castillo, Marq to his friends, crossed his arms over his chest and waited for the litany to end. "Call my mother whatever you like, you little shit. But get off my property or I'm calling the cops."

"I thought you were some kind of bad-ass boss. Mister ex-con with your prison tattoos. You're nothing but a pussy. A spineless little pussy-man, hiding behind the police," sneered the waiter.

Marq felt the rage rising in him, stiffening his spine and forming a quaking knot in his gut. Part of him begged to plant a fist in the twenty-two year old kid's jaw. Back when Marq himself was twenty-two, that is exactly what he would have done. But he had learned. There were better ways to deal with hotheads like the one in front of him. He lowered his voice to a soft purr, almost smiling as he spoke. "Look, José, the rules of the job are simple. Show up on time. Follow directions. No stealing. No drugs. You're zero for four. This is your last warning. Leave now or explain to the cops about the weed in your pocket and extra sixty bucks you skimmed from my register just now when you thought I wasn't looking. Consider it your severance. You have thirty seconds."

With one final kick at the dumpster, José turned and stalked off toward the end of the alley. Marq let out a pent-up breath and followed at a slow pace to make sure the guy really left.

He rounded the corner onto the sidewalk that ran in front of his restaurant and scanned up and down the Boulevard. He spotted the bright green T-shirt half a block away, its wearer still visibly seething as he shoved past pedestrians on the sidewalk.

Damn. He should have made the kid take off the T-shirt first. Nothing like advertising your business on the back of a pissed-off, high-flying, violent troublemaker.

He was about to turn back inside, when he heard an unmistakably feminine howl of rage. His heart skipped a beat, and Marq took off at a jog.

He found the lady sprawled on her butt on the sidewalk, cradling one foot on her lap. She had obviously just come from the beach, with a bright-colored biking peeking out from under one of those itty-bitty dresses that passed for cover ups. Sprawled the way she was on the ground, it didn't cover much. Her legs were long and toned and tanned, and the top of her dress had slipped down to reveal a round breast barely contained in its skimpy triangle of fabric.

"Do you need a hand?"

A low growl of feminine outrage was his response.

"What happened?" He spotted a tote bag a few feet away, with odds and ends of the kind of junk women carried in their bags spilling onto the concrete.

"What does it look like happened. Some jackass just shoved me down."

Marq stuffed what he could see back in the bag and then turned back to the woman on the ground. She looked red in the face, her long brown hair clung to her sweaty temples. She met his gaze with a pair of brown eyes the color of roasted cacao nibs, and furious expression that promised doom and dismemberment to anyone nearby.

Shit. José hadn't just taken off with his cash, but also assaulted a potential customer while still wearing the restaurant uniform. Just what he needed, a lawsuit. He could feel the flush of anger and shame crawling up the back of his neck as he tried to gather every ounce of wit and charm he could muster to fix the situation.

Her eyes finally focused on his for what must have been the first time, and they flew wide. "Marquez Castillo de Florez."

He blinked at the use of his full name, and he stiffened instinctively like a naughty kid called out by his mother. He searched her face again, trying to place her.

"It is you, isn't it? It's me, Kelsie." She gave him a half-smile, and tried to surreptitiously wipe the tears from her eyes with the back of one arm.

The moment the words were out of her mouth, Marq felt like an idiot for not recognizing her. She was Kelsie Forrester, the baby sister of his best friend from high school. He had known her since she was about three years old. "Kelsie. Jesus. Let me help you up."

He gave her the bag and then held out his hand and pulled her to her feet. She shifted her weight to one leg. Before he could ask about her obviously injured foot, she flung her arms around his neck.

Tentatively, Marq set his arms on the backs of her shoulders. On somewhere safe. The Kelsie Forrester in his arms was no longer the chubby-cheeked, bright-eyed little girl of twelve that he had last seen well over a dozen years ago. She had grown taller, slimmer, womanly. Her breasts pushed against his chest, and his hands touched smooth, warm skin. She smelled of citrus and sunscreen, and his body reacted instinctively to the shape and scent of her.

Gently, he pushed back and looked down at her. Not as far down as he used to in high school, when the top of her head barely crested his chest and he could hold snatched toys up out of her reach. He might have a whole three inches on her now, and in high heels, they would stand eye-to-eye.

He frowned as he looked down at her yellow-painted toes. The one looked angry and red with a drop of what he feared was blood trickling down onto the pavement. "You're bleeding."

"The jerk who shoved past me stepped on my foot."

He cringed, silently cursing José for what he hoped was the last time. "Where are your shoes?"

Her eyes shifted away for a second before her smile returned to him, tighter than it had been a minute ago. "It's a long story. Um, I need to sit down for a minute."

"In here." He held out an arm and led her through the bistro tables that led to the front door of the restaurant.

She half walked, half hopped along with him, but stopped short of the door and tugged on his arm. "Here on the patio is fine."

"Wouldn't you rather go inside and cool off?" Her face had turned an even brighter shade of red, and he could see where dirt streaked her dress from the fall.

She shook her head and motioned down to her feet. "No shoes, no service, right? Besides, I don't want to get you in trouble."

He paused. "In trouble?"

"Are you on your break or something?" She gave a pointed look at his T-shirt. His had the same *Chocolate, Chocolate* logo on the front that the rest of his employees wore, though his T-shirt was black instead of the bright green.

"It's no trouble. I promise." He grinned at her.

Their gazes caught for several long heartbeats. Heartbeats where he drank in her wide eyes, her wary smile. The pupils that seemed to darken, just barely. He thought he saw speculation in that smile, plus something else that made his breath hitch and his groin tighten.

He nearly groaned before rational thought returned and he remembered that the hottie he was ogling was *Kelsie*. Rob Forrester's baby sister. If Rob, or Rob's brother Helmut, had the slightest inkling of what Marq's lower half had been contemplating just now, they would bury him. The Forresters took care of each other, as Marq knew all too well. He had the tattoos on his arms to prove it.

The memory chilled him, and he gave Kelsie a hard look. She shrank back a fraction at whatever she read in his eyes, her chin tilting, questioning. He turned away. "Wait here, I will be right back in two minutes."

Marq stalked inside the space that was his pride, his dream. The décor was all cool stainless steel with industrial accents and occasional bursts of bright colors. The menu, which he had created himself, was much the same. Polished, edgy, with a few surprises. Surprises like the decadent baked goods, and the ways he featured chocolate or cocoa in even his savory dishes. He blended chocolate with spicy peppers for *mole* sauces, unsweetened cocoa with salt and coconuts to crust fresh caught fish. Raw cacao beans, white chocolate, even cocoa butter was used in unusual ways in every dish on his menu. So far, the foodie community in Palm Beach loved it. Not bad for a kid from the worst barrio this side of Miami.

He quickly jogged back to the back room for a first aid kit and fished a pair of Croc's out of the lost and found. On his way back to the patio, he poured a glass of ice water in the kitchen, and briefly filled in his pastry assistant, Sofia, about what happened. She cut him a slice of thick fudgy brownie from the pan she was icing and put it on a plate for Marq to take outside.

When he set the items in front of Kelsie, he watched her eyes widen in surprise and joy, but then narrow. She shook her head. "I can't."

"Sure you can. Brownies are the house specialty. And the shoes have been sitting in the back for over a month. Whichever tourist dropped them isn't coming back. One of the kitchen staff is calling you a cab to take you home. Now give me your foot."

She flashed him an alarmed look, but he ignored it and found a Band-Aid and antibiotic ointment in his kit. He tried to put on his most patient expression and nudged the glass of water closer. "You drink, I'll clean."

Reluctantly, she accepted water, and took a long sip. She sighed and lifted up her foot. Marq cradled it gently in one hand and tried to ignore the glimpse of upper thigh where her dress rode up. She stiffened as he wipe the cut down with antiseptic. He winced, seeing the first signs of a bruise forming. "There, all done."

She set the foot down and slipped it into the shoes he'd given her, then looked at the brownie again. "Really. Marq, I, um, well..."

"Well what?"

"You're being so kind to me. Its' just...I don't have any money with me. To pay for the brownie. Or the cab."

He must have frowned, because she looked away, pretending to admire the bougainvillea that lined the borders of the patio. The look on her face reminded him of one time when she was maybe seven or eight and got caught...doing something. He didn't know what. But she looked guilty and ashamed.

"How did you come to be walking the streets of Palm Beach, barefoot and without any money?"

She eyed the brownie. He nudged it toward her. He could see her lips moving.

"Do you promise not to laugh at me?"

"I promise. If you promise to eat a few bites. My treat. The cab, too. You're not walking anywhere with your foot like that."

She looked so longingly at the dessert that he almost laughed out loud for joy. But as her story of the afternoon's events unfolded in between bites of chocolate, a blush stained her cheeks darker and darker. Marq could feel the coil of tension inside him winding tighter and tighter.

He alternated between wanting to throttle the jerk who left her stranded at the beach with no money and no shoes, and wanting to lecture her about protecting herself. But then the last bite of chocolate disappeared into her mouth and he found himself mesmerized by the sight of her licking the frosting off her fork. His mouth went dry as his thoughts immediately conjured the image of her licking *him* with that same rapturous expression on her face.

Damn.

Just then the cab pulled up to the curb. He stood up from the table and turned so abruptly that he knocked his chair over, hoping the apron slung around his waist would disguise the erection he hadn't been able to control.

She stood up a little slower and pulled her tote bag over one shoulder. "Thank you, Marq. For all of your help. I owe you, big time."

He almost laughed at that, but the sound came out more like a cross between a snort and a cough. If only she knew just how much her family already owed him. There was no reason to drag all that up here, now, with her. She was just a kid when it happened.

He gave her what he hoped passed for a benign smile and handed the cab driver a stack of bills to get her safely back out of his life.

CHAPTER TWO

A blast of steamy Florida air washed over Kelsie where she sat on the sofa of her mother's house. She looked up from the novel she spent all afternoon reading. She glanced at the clock. No, the novel that she had spent all afternoon and most of the evening reading.

She heard her mother's voice at the front door. Kelsie set the book down and stood and stretched, wincing as her sore, Band-Aid-ed feet touched the cool terracotta tile of the floor. "Do you need help with something, mom?"

She hobbled toward the foyer, stopping when she realized that her mother was not alone.

Edna Forrester stood in the open doorway wearing her favorite summer dress as she chatted with a man Kelsie didn't recognize. He was bald with a paunch and a wrinkled linen suit and he was holding her mother's hand to his lips.

"Good night, Willard," Edna said and

closed the door softly after him. The glowing smile on her face dimmed as she spotted her daughter.

"Were you on a date?"

The remains of her mother's smile vanished and her lips thinned into a hard line. Edna sat down on the hall bench and carefully bent to remove her shoes, not answering.

"Mom, who was that?"

"His name is Willard Jansen."

Kelsie offered a hand to help her mother up, but Edna waved her off and used the arm of the bench to push herself to standing.

"How is your hip?"

Edna shot her a quelling glance. "Fine, thank you."

Kelsie followed her mother to the kitchen and watched her sort through today's mail. When Edna sighed at the dirty plates on the counter, Kelsie winced. "Here, let me clean those up."

But her mom waived her off, leaving Kelsie to watch, silently as her mother cleaned up after her.

Finally, she couldn't take it any longer. "Aren't you even going to ask what happened? How I got home? Whether I'm okay?"

Her mom raised one eyebrow. "Did something happen?"

A sob crept into Kelsie's throat. "I guess you didn't get my message? I got stranded at the beach. Zack just left me there alone. And then I hurt my foot, and...and...are you even listening to me?"

Edna looked up from the dishwasher where she was loading Kelsie's dinner dishes. "You are here. You seem fine. As for the how, well, it looks like you figured something out."

Kelsie took a step backwards at the frostiness in her mother's voice.

"Kelsie, I love you. But you are twenty-five years old. You're about to graduate from law school, for heaven's sake. I shouldn't need to check up on you like you're a teenager. And I don't need you waiting up for me."

This wasn't the first time they'd had this argument. Kelsie had her own apartment near campus in Miami but always left for the summer so she could stay with her mother. Helmut was always calling and asking how Mom was, and he got crabby if Kelsie hadn't talked to her in a while. And over the past few years, her health had gotten worse. Not horrible, but she had hip surgery and then a twisted ankle and she really did need help around the house some days. Kelsie loved her childhood home, but it had four bedrooms and a big yard and was just way too much for one person living alone.

And then there was Mom's bad habit of not answering her cell phone. Helmut would kill her if he couldn't get ahold of their mother. Worse, he would move back in himself, and then all three of them would be at each other's throats.

Though Edna never complained about having Kelsie around, lately she had been making more and more pointed comments about when the fall semester started. And when Kelsie planned to move back to her own place.

"Don't you even want to hear who paid for my cab ride home?"

Edna rolled her eyes and finished loading the dishes into the dishwasher.

"Marq Castillo."

She watched with some satisfaction as her mother paused, the plate in her hand quavering as though she might drop it.

"Oh?" asked mom with an indifference that Kelsie could tell was fake.

"I haven't seen him in forever. He is working at some fancy new restaurant down on the strip. Chocolate, Chocolate was the name. Doesn't surprise me. Do you remember how he was always offering to cook when he came over? He made more cookies than you did when I was a kid." The words tumbled out of her mouth fast, excited to share her news.

"I see."

"He was really nice to me today. Found me a pair of shoes, bought me some food. Called me a cab. I always wondered why he and Rob never kept in touch after...after everything they went through."

Edna's face had closed down, almost sick looking. She looked pained. Stiff. Her hands clutched a dishtowel like it was a life preserver.

"Mom? What's the matter? Do you feel okay? Maybe you should sit down." She made to grab the towel, but her mother pulled it back and clutched it to her chest.

"No, I'm fine. Honey, about Marq Castillo..."

Kelsie waited for several long heartbeats for her mother to continue. When she did, her words had a cold edge.

"Stay away from him. That boy is trouble. Big trouble."

"Man."

"Hmm?" asked Edna, startled out of her reverie.

"Marq isn't a boy anymore. He's the same age as Rob. He must be almost thirty."

Her mother looked every inch the Southern society matron in that moment. Her short silver hair looked like she had just left the salon. Her floral sundress was unwrinkled and fresh. Her makeup flawless. So when she snorted, Kelsie couldn't help but take note.

"He was a trouble maker. He dragged Rob into a heap of trouble, too. Trust me, boys like him don't grow up to be men. They grow up to be bigger boys who get in even bigger trouble."

"Drop it, Kelsie. It's none of your business." Helmut's voice sounded calm. Deceptively calm. How could he sound so calm?

"My family is none of my business? You planning your wedding and not even inviting Rob is none of my business?" She could hear her voice getting shriller and shriller, and she didn't care. "He is your brother, Helmut. Did you even call him?"

"He hasn't taken a call from me in years. You should have heard what he told me when I tried to invite him to your high school graduation."

"Was that the last time you tried? Eight years ago?"

Kelsie stared at the phone, wishing Helmut were there in person. So she could throttle him. "How old are you, anyway. Forty-four or fourteen?"

"Enough. I will talk to you later." Just like that, he ended the call.

She glared at the phone, wishing she had someone to talk to. Her mother was out again, off to play bridge. Or was tonight her water aerobics? Or her book club? Or her dinner club? Or maybe she was out on another date with Willard. Her mother had more of a social life than she herself did. She was glad. Of course she was. And not the least bit jealous.

In fact, Kelsie was thrilled for her.

Ecstatic.

The woman was probably hiding from her sadness and anger over her sons' feud. Pretending that all was well, even though her two boys wouldn't speak to each other. Her mother had lost her husband and then raised three children on her own. Well, technically, only two children had needed raising. Helmut had already left for college when Daddy had his heart attack. The woman deserved to enjoy life a little. Kelsie just wished that today, right this minute, that Edna would take a little time away from her social life and pay attention to her family.

She wished that her mother would force Rob and Helmut to start talking again.

She may as well wish for a flying horse.

The family feud it started when Rob was in high school. Kelsie was eleven or twelve at the time. Helmut was living in Chicago. He had a serious girlfriend up there who he'd brought home once, and who Mom was sure he was going to marry. Kelsie didn't remember much about that girlfriend, just that she laughed a lot and was the only person who had ever tried playing the piano that Mom kept in the front room, the "parlor". Then Helmut was in a bad car accident and the girlfriend died, and he came back home for a couple of weeks, moody and irritable.

Rob and his friend Marq were inseparable back then. Kelsie loved it when the two of them hung out at their house. At the time, she was at an awkward age of twelve, full of self-doubt and pre-teen angst.

And she was madly in love with her brother's best friend.

To her eyes, Marq was devastatingly handsome in a devil-may-care, swashbuckling pirate sort of way. He was wiry and tall, with the gauntness of a youth who hadn't yet filled in around his frame. But his shoulders were square and broad, and she once caught a glimpse of him shirtless. So she knew that he had six-pack abs and toned arms and shoulders. His hair was deep black, a little too long, and a little too un-kempt some days. He was deeply tan, tanner than she would ever be, and he walked with a lilting swagger that made her knees go weak.

The boys spent hours and hours holed up in Rob's room, or out under the shade of the an-cient live oaks in the grove behind their house. There were other guys that hung around the house, too--Rob's basketball teammates, Marq's cousin Joaquín, some others whose names she never caught.

Her favorite days were the ones where Marq would stay the night. That spring when her brothers had their biggest fight, Marq stayed over a lot. Every weekend and sometimes dur-ing the week. He and Rob would eat anything they could find in the fridge, and their mother was always complaining about the grocery bills.

But oh, the boy could cook.

If Kelsie woke up early enough on a Saturday or Sunday morning, she could usually find Marq sitting wide awake on the living room couch. Rob would be snoring till after eleven if no one kicked him out of bed. She never understood why Marq didn't just go home rather than sit alone in someone else's house, but she never complained. Not once.

Because he would make her breakfast. Scrambled eggs, chocolate chip pancakes, sometimes grilled cheese with bacon or fried dough sprinkled with cinnamon and sugar. Kelsie would perch on a stool at the breakfast counter, and Marq would put on one of her mother's floral aprons. He would juggle the eggs before cracking them, or play tricks with the gas stove to make a small fireball. Anything to make her giggle. He would serve her breakfast with a smile and a bow, and drape her napkin in her lap and talk with a bad French accent, or else toss the pancakes straight from the griddle to her plate.

He made her feel special.

But when Helmut came home to recover from his accident and grieve for his lost fiancée, the mood in the house shifted. He picked fights with Rob, and constantly complained to their mother about his brother's poor life decisions.

The day of the big fight, Kelsie woke up early and had gone down to the kitchen, hoping to find Marq, but he wasn't there. Rob had several friends over the night before, and they were all sleeping soundly hours after they were normally up and about.

Years later, she would recognize the bits of pottery, profusion of Ziploc bags, and the sweet scent of illegal trouble.

But at age twelve, all Kelsie recognized was that she couldn't expect chocolate chip pancakes that morning. Marq never cooked for her when other boys were around, no matter how early he woke up. He wouldn't even make eye contact with her. So, having given up hope for another special breakfast, she grabbed a book and headed out to the trees behind the house to read.

It was after noon when she heard the raised voices from the house. She climbed down out of her tree and skipped back toward the kitchen to see what was going on. The next thing she knew, Helmut had Marq by the collar of his T-shirt and practically shoved him out the front door. There was so much shouting. Helmut and Rob shouting at each other. Mom shouting at both of them. All three shouting at Kelsie to mind her own business.

Rob left after Marq and didn't come home that night. After all the yelling, the silence in the house was deafening. Helmut and Edna ignored each other with pointed intensity, and Kelsie buried herself in her book again and avoided them both. Late the following night, the phone rang and Edna left. The next morning, she brought Rob home with his arm in a sling.

There had been a car accident. Several of the guys in the car got hurt pretty badly, worse than just a broken arm. One died. Not Marq, obviously.

Rob graduated from high school just a couple of months later and left for college. By then he had quit shouting at Helmut. He'd quit talking at all. Marq never came over anymore, either.

That summer was unbearable. Helmut went home to Chicago, back to his job and his grown-up life. Rob packed up for college and never looked back. And Edna and Kelsie were left alone together in their big, empty house.

Things were never the same after that.

She looked around her bedroom for something to hurl. Not the phone--she needed that intact. Not any of the little china figurines that lined her shelves. Those were treasures from childhood. Her father had begun bringing those to her for birthdays and Christmas, and her brothers had continued the tradition.

With a growl, she threw herself on the bed. For some reason, when she talked to Helmut, she always felt about sixteen years old. Maybe it was because he always treated her like

a child. And maybe *that* was because he had rescued her from more than one childish scrape
over the years. So how was it that the man could
act so mature and responsible when it came to
her well-being, but turned into a stubborn teenager himself when it came to their brother?

She picked up one of the decorative pil-
lows--a frilly heart-shaped one that she had
cross-stitched in the sixth grade--and threw it at
the wall. Hard. Too hard. The pillow ricocheted
and smashed into the corner of the shelf of figurines.

She watched in horror as they tottered,
and one began to fall.

"No!" With a cry, she raced towards the
wall to catch the tumbling statue, but it crashed
onto the tile floor, just beyond the edge of the
area rug. Kelsie fell to her knees next to the pieces, and gathered them up.

The figure had been Sleeping Beauty, collapsed on her bed, asleep and awaiting rescue by
her dashing Prince Charming. Dad had bought it
for her when she was six. He fingers shook as
she tried to gently test the bits to see how bad
the damage was. To see if she could glue the
pieces back together.

The tears that poured down her cheeks
made it hard to see clearly, and the little trinket
had been broken in far too many pieces.

Kelsie took in a deep, shuddering breath
and heaped all of the broken china into the palm

of one hand. She cradled the pieces as she walked through her mother's house to the kitchen in search of a bag where she could store them. Maybe with the right glue and a whole lot of patience, she could restore the thing to the way it was.

Kelsie didn't need to sit around and wait for her mother to fix things for her. She could patch up the family troubles herself. She just needed a plan to bring her brothers together. If she could just get them in the same room, she was sure she could get them to talk to each other. To laugh together. To be a family again.

She closed the zipper on her baggie of broken princess parts and reached for a pad of paper. She needed a plan. And an ally.

CHAPTER THREE

"Are you ready for it, ladies?" With a grin and a flourish, Marq dipped the rim of a martini glass in chocolate shavings and then filled it with his restaurant's signature cocktail and handed it to a beaming brunette wearing a plastic tiara.

If his old high school buddies could see him now, toasting bachelorettes and serving chocolate mousse artistically drizzled with raspberry sauce, or any of the other over-the-top concoctions on tonight's menu, they would probably try to drag him out to the back alley for a thorough beating.

"Open up for me, my dear." He popped a chocolate kiss into the waiting mouth of the bachelorette, and grinned wickedly as her coterie of friends all chortled with delight.

His old high school buddies could go to hell. If they weren't there already. The thought was sobering. A couple of the guys from his block had died or gone to prison. Hell, Marq himself did four years in juvenile detention and then another two in a low-security prison for breaking parole. And then there was Joaquín.

He looked around the glittering room full of fat, happy, rich folks. Pride battled with a nagging sense of guilt. He'd gotten lucky. So damn lucky he still couldn't believe it. By all rights, he should have been another statistic. Another Latino gang banger from the wrong part of town, living down to everyone's expectations.

He paused in the dining room to refill a glass of water for one guest, then help clean a table, wincing as the bus boy haphazardly tossed the plates onto the plastic tray. He nearly bit his tongue attempting to keep from lecturing the kid on the cost of dishware. Instead, he plastered a smile on his face, gave him a quick pat on the shoulder and said, "Great job. You got this."

He needed a break before he started sounding like his *abuela*.

Marq stopped by the dessert display case and scooped a handful of the pecans that they used for garnish onto a clean plate and headed back towards his office off the kitchen to put his feet up for a few minutes.

It was the silky swath of bare skin that caught his attention. Perched at the bar was a brunette with a killer back, smooth and tanned and bare nearly to her waist.

If she hadn't turned around, he might

have kept on walking. He might have contented himself with ogling the sinuous line of her spine. The curve of her neck where it disappeared under one of those womanly piles of hair. The way her earrings brushed the tops of bared shoulders, sparkling under the decorator-aligned spot lights. He might have simply looked his fill and disappeared into his office alone to enjoy his snack and the memory of the zing of lust he had just enjoyed.

But she turned. And his breath caught again as he recognized her profile, the sparkle in her eyes. Kelsie. A hot flush crept up from his collar as he realized that for the second time in a week, he had gotten all hot and bothered over her.

Then she smiled at him, and gave a small, hopeful wave. He couldn't have ignored her if he had wanted to.

"You won't believe how silly I felt when I called earlier today to find out when your next shift was," she said as he settled into the barstool next to hers. "I think the hostess thought I was joking when I said I wasn't sure whether you were a waiter or a disher or what."

"Heh." Marq studied the lines of her face as she spoke, just a little too quickly. She always started like that when they were kids, he remembered. Just a little too fast, like she was afraid to talk to him. Like she was afraid *of* him.

"I am impressed, Marq. Really impressed.

When did you open the place?"

"Right before Valentine's Day," he said. He could almost feel his ego swelling at her words. Maybe other parts beyond his ego were swelling as well. "I managed to get a big write-up in the paper because of all the chocolate."

"Oh. I guess I missed it. I live down in Miami during the school year."

"College, right? What's your major?"

Her eyes flickered down to her glass, where her finger traced a swirl in the condensation that had beaded up on the side. She gave what seemed like a quick inhale, like she was bracing herself for something. "Law."

He let out a breath he didn't realize he'd been holding. "That would not have been my first guess."

Her eyes narrowed on him. "Why do you say that?"

He sat back at the sudden burst of fury he sensed behind her words. He shook his head, the lamest possible reply. "I don't know. I guess I just expected you to study something...lighter. More fun. I can't see you burying yourself in an office with your nose in a stuffy book."

She let out a little huff.

"Okay. Well, I guess I don't have much experience with lawyers." *Except from being on the wrong side of the courtroom.* "Doesn't that kind of degree take years to finish?"

"The J.D., or Juris Doctor degree takes

seven years. Or more. Four in undergrad. Three in graduate school. I graduate next May. And I like stuffy books." She picked up her glass and took one last sip, then pulled a tiny wallet out of her tiny purse and handed him a couple of bills.

"For the cab ride the other day. Thank you."

He pushed the money back. "It was my pleasure to help out an old friend."

Marq watched as she slid off the barstool and made to leave. She looked stunning. Her dress was sexy as hell. It covered everything in front from her collarbone to just above her knees, but flowed and clung in just the right places to prove that she was a woman and not a little girl. And he knew that the back of the dress was cut sinfully low, dipping just below her waist to tease him about the luscious skin underneath.

God, he was such a fool. And she was far, far too good for him. Too beautiful. Too smart. Too closely related to the men who had ruined his life.

Her brothers had been responsible for getting him sent to jail. Without the older brother's influence, especially, he might have been let go with just a warning or a few months as a juvenile offender for a very minor crime.

Instead, while they were off at college, he was rubbing elbows with the worst of Florida's scum.

Kelsie shot him one last look. Her eyes were unreadable. Bright, blackened pupils. Pain or intent? It was like she tried to force a thousand thoughts his way, but he didn't have the first clue what she was trying to tell him.

"Wait." He touched her hand. Soft, lithe. Her hands were slender and strong, used to books and pens and keyboards, not to the sanitizing dishwater of a kitchen or the inevitable burns and cuts that came with commercial food service. "Look, I'm a jerk. I haven't seen you in so long, and so much has changed. Can we start over? Have a drink with me."

Every nerve in Kelsie's body zinged with pleasure. She took another small sip of the cocktail Marq had ordered for her. The liquid was dark, rich, and tasted of coffee and chocolate and cream. It rolled over her tongue and warmed her through to her core. The drink was, she realized, the exact shade of his eyes. Dark, decadent, and dangerous.

Her mother's warning echoed in her head but her body thrummed with the promise of forbidden fruit.

His restaurant T-shirt hugged the muscles of his shoulders and revealed corded biceps and powerful forearms. A tattoo circled just above one elbow, and on his other arm, another design nearly trailed from the hem of his sleeve to his wrist. She wondered what they meant to him. She had an almost irresistible urge to trace the swirling black and red designs with her fingertips.

He was telling her a story about something funny that happened in the kitchen. A mix-up of ingredients, and the horrified reaction of one of the waiters when they realized the mistake. She laughed, and their gazes caught, not for the first time that evening.

A smile split his face and brightened it from his eyes to the hard lines of his jaw. He looked so relaxed, just for that moment. So open. So beautiful.

Her breath caught in her throat, and she couldn't look away. Not when he wrapped his fingers around hers, cradling them in his grip. His skin was rough, hard, used to work. So different from her soft, manicured ones. His touch was hot on hers.

The club where they sat was only a few doors down from Marq's restaurant. Back in his place, he had muttered something about the peanut gallery before tossing his apron on the bar and offering his arm for the quick stroll. A jazz band played, the music washing over Kelsie and forcing her and Marq to sit closer to hear each other. His breath tickled her ear. "Dance with me."

He pulled her to the dance floor and drew

her close. Hard up against his body, his hand light but hot on her hip. She glanced up at his jaw, his ear, the line of his hair, dark and curling over his temple. He smelled of soap but with an undertone of spice. The *chile* he used in so many of his recipes. She let out a pent up breath slowly, savoring the feel of his arms around her.

"I still can't believe that it's you I'm dancing with," he whispered.

She looked, first at his lips, so close to her own. She drew her gaze up to his eyes and felt breathless. "Why is that?"

He laughed. Low, rueful. "Because the last time I saw you, you were a little kid with those big chocolate eyes that used to follow us around. And now you're..."

She was liquid fire. She was fairly purring at the heat between their bodies. "I am what?"

"All grown up."

Kelsie could feel the heat that began in her core, heat that seared her breasts where they brushed against his chest, where it crept up her cheeks. His hand at her hip traced around to her lower back, found the opening of her dress. She gasped as his fingers touched the bare skin there, lightly tracing her vertebrae.

She needed to think. Dear God, his hands were making it hard for her to think. "Marq."

His eyes flickered back up to hers. His pupils were deep black pools in the dim light of the dance floor. "Mmmm?"

She inched backwards from him. Just barely. Just enough so that she could breathe without feeling the heat of his chest through her silk top. Just enough for a few brain cells to begin working again. "I need..."

He trailed his fingers brushed her lower back again, leaving sparkling trails of pure sensation in their wake.

She nearly melted.

"What is it you need?"

She inhaled and tried to steady her breathing. "I need a favor."

All the languid heat in his body seemed to freeze at her words. His jaw, the set of his shoulders, even the hand at the small of her back just locked up tight. His eyes flashed. "What kind of a favor?"

She felt she must have crossed a line somewhere and she drew back another inch, lifting her head higher. "I know we haven't known each other very long. Well, I mean...we've known each other forever. But we just met again and..."

"What kind of a favor, Kelsie?

She flinched at the words. She felt the heat rise in her cheeks and knew it wasn't just the alcohol making her blush. She was in trouble and she knew it. Her whole idea was stupid.

Still, she hadn't chosen law as a career because she was afraid to plead her case. And she could talk to anyone, convince anyone of anything. Charm anyone. Charming this man shouldn't be so tough.

"Do you need money? What is it?"

She schooled her features into what she hoped was a disarming smile. "Nothing like that. It's about my brother."

His eyes flicked open in what she thought was surprise, then narrowed. "Which brother?"

"Both of them, actually. I know you haven't talked to Rob in a long time. He and Helmut never talk. I mean never. They haven't spoken a word in years. Both of them barely talk to me, either. I hate the whole situation. Helmut's getting married and won't even invite Rob. I think they're both being a pair of jackasses and that it's far past time that they grew up and got over it." She cringed, hearing the tumble of words fall out of her mouth with too much emotion and too little confidence.

Marq shrugged. "So what does that have to do with me? I'm not exactly on speaking terms with them either."

That didn't surprise her at all.

"I don't know what all happened between you guys back in school, but I do know that it was pretty bad. Bad enough that my mother warned me away from you the other day."

"Oh yeah?" His tone had changed to something less wary and way more predatory.

She was still in his arms, one of her arms around his shoulder. So it took so very little effort to tease her fingers into the hair at the nape of his neck. To guide his head down as she lifted her lips toward his. To do exactly what she had fantasized about when she was twelve years old. To kiss Marq.

She could have been coy and just brushed closed lips against his.

But a dozen years' worth of fantasy merited way more than a little girl's peck on the lips. He tasted like beer and chocolate and forbidden fruit. With a groan, he opened his mouth and then she wasn't sure who was kissing who.

The kiss could have lasted a second or an hour. She lost all sense of time or place until the music quieted and the both drew back, breathless.

Kelsie took his hand and led him back toward their table.

"I have a proposal for you," she said as he held her chair for her to sit down.

Marq gave her a wolfish grin. "If it involves another kiss like that last one, I'm in."

"Um," Kelsie grasped for words. "Yes, sort of. But not really. This is about my brothers, remember."

"I don't want to kiss your brothers."

She laughed. "I have a plan that I think might get both Rob and Helmut talking. To each other."

His eyes hardened.

"You see, they can both be a little overprotective. Each in their own way."

Marq nodded. "Doesn't surprise me."

"I think that if they both think that I am in some kind of trouble, that they will come rescue me. My mom gave me the idea."

Marq drew back and his eyes narrowed. "I'm not entirely sure I follow."

"You. My mother thinks you're dangerous. Helmut thinks I'm helpless. And Rob used to be your best friend and generally disagrees with anything Helmut says. If they all think that you and I...that we are together..."

He blew out a breath and a shadow crossed his face. Then he smirked. "You want me to start a family war for you."

"No!" Kelsie chewed her lip. "Well, yes, maybe. I guess I do."

Marq downed the rest of his drink in one gulp, then smiled.

"I will think about it."

Relief washed over her and she sipped the last bit of her own cocktail.

"But first, I think I need another dance."

Marq frowned over the numbers on his computer screen. The accounting side of the business would never be his favorite part. He had hired an accountant to set up the electronic bookkeeping system and keep everything in or-

der. The system worked great. But it still required Marq to look over things occasionally.

It looked like the business was firmly in
the black. He made nice profits from the bar,
from the bakery, from the restaurant menu. His
party room was booked well in advance with
bridal showers, rehearsal dinners, corporate
events. His paycheck was steady for the first
time in his life.

If he wasn't careful, all this success was
going to bore him to death.

A shadow fell over his desk. He looked
up and grinned. Salvation had just arrived.

Kelsie stood before him with a gleam in
her eye that seemed to promise mischief. A black
tank skimmed the tops of her breasts and clung
to the curves of her waistline, baring just a hint
of her tanned bellybutton. Denim shorts caressed curvy hips, cut high on her thighs, leading his eyes up to that hot core between her legs.

"I hope you don't mind that I didn't re-
turn your text message earlier today," she said.
"But I figured my answer would be better given
in person."

He had forced himself to wait a full 48
hours after they said goodbye at the club before
calling. Two full sleepless nights filled with the
memory of her body, her scent, her whispers.
Two cold showers. One pitiful solo hand job that
couldn't take the edge off his longing. Two days
of hoping that she wanted him. That she wasn't

just using him for her crazy revenge plot. That she wasn't mad that he didn't agree on the spot to make himself a target for the Forrester brother's ire. That he could hold her in his arms and taste her again.

When can I see you again? He worried over the words as he typed them. Worried that she would see right through a dinner invitation, would scorn anything more blunt. He cringed at the simple message as he hit the send button.

Now here she was.

He was around his desk in two quick strides. She met him half way, grabbing a fistful of his T-shirt and dragging him into her arms.

Kelsie's breasts pressed against Marq's chest, her nipples hard little buds that teased his own overheated flesh. Her head was tilted back, resting on the brick of his office wall, offering him full access to her sleek, sensitive neck. He tasted her, and she gasped, clinging to his shoulders as though she might fall.

He ran one hand down her hip and curled his fingers around the curve of her bottom, finding the bare skin of the back of her thigh just below the hem of too-short shorts. She shivered and shifted against him, brushing her pelvis up against the erection that strained at his jeans.

With a groan, he grasped her leg and hooked it up and around his back, nestling himself closer.

He had no intention of letting her fall.

He used the wall as an anchor, rubbed his thigh between hers and groaned again as she arched against him. Her fingers tangled in his hair and she pulled his mouth back up to hers. Their lips parted. Their tongues intertwined. Their pulses beat together in an erratic, frantic tempo. His hand found her abdomen then up to the swell of her breast, bare except for the flimsy fabric of her tank top.

Damn, he loved the thick steamy heat of the South Florida summer.

His thumb had just found her nipple, making her moan into his mouth. Then he heard the doorknob rattle behind them.

They stilled. He ripped his mouth from hers. Her breath was ragged, her lips parted and swollen from their kiss. Her pupils were dark, liquid pools of black. Of desire. For him.

"Just a minute," he managed to say over his shoulder in the general direction of the door. Carefully he helped lower her to the floor and made sure she looked steady on her feet before he stepped back.

She smiled, a ghost of a smile that looked drowsy and bashful. "You should probably go. They need you."

He jerked his head back toward the frosted glass of the restaurant office door. Someone's silhouette filled the other side. "Probably."

"I'm sorry. I shouldn't have stopped by while you were working."

"Don't apologize. And don't go any-where."

He opened the office door and found the bartender, Julie, with her arms crossed over her chest, tapping one foot impatiently. She looked over his shoulder, then back at him, one eye-brow raised, but didn't say anything. She hand-ed him a fat stack of bills with a white slip of pa-per wrapped around them. "The till was full. For the safe."

He nodded, put the report slip on his desk and stuffed the money in the special timed safe that he kept in his office. The safe plus the special armored car service that carried the cash to the bank for him cost more than he had ex-pected when he first opened his own business. But he'd been to prison. Heard talk from guys doing hard time for robbing places like this. He took no chances on safety.

"Are you coming back to the dining room tonight? Or are you otherwise engaged?" Julie asked, throwing Kelsie another unreadable look.

Marq shrugged and looked at his watch. "It's nearly closing time. Unless there are any VIP's out there, I'd rather stay here and, uh..." He felt the jab to his ribs as Kelsie stepped up beside him.

"We're just catching up on old times. I've known Marq since I was little. Old family friend. Kelsie." She extended her hand toward Julie.

Julie seemed to study the proffered hand

for a moment before wiping her own off on her apron and shaking it. "Julie Alvarez. I'm also an old family friend. I've never seen you in here before."

Marq explained, "Julie was my first employee when I opened the restaurant, and she's one hell of a bartender. She keeps me in line."

Kelsie smiled. "You said you're a family friend? Did you go to school with Marq? Maybe you know my brother Rob?"

A shadow passed over Julie's face. "Rob Forrester?"

Tension crawled up Marq's spine at the ice in Julie's voice, but Kelsie continued on as if she didn't notice. "Yes. Rob Forrester."

Julie's features froze. "I was Joaquín's fiancée."

He took a step forward, putting his body slightly between the two women. Kelsie quirked an eyebrow at him, clearly not connecting the dots.

"Who's covering the bar, Julie?" Marq asked through gritted teeth.

Julie turned on her heel and left without another word.

"Who is Joaquín?" Kelsie asked.

He blew out a breath as Julie retreated to her domain behind the counter. He took an additional second to gather his wits before facing Kelsie. "Joaquín was my cousin. He went to school with Rob and me. He died."

Her lips, still swollen from his kisses parted in an O and her eyes softened with concern. "I'm sorry."

Good God, she doesn't know about Joaquín.

He pulled her into his arms. She buried her face against his chest, and he realized that, no matter their size difference, she was trying to hold *him*. To comfort *him*. He couldn't remember the last time someone had done that.

He ran a finger down her cheek and lifted her chin and nearly drowned in her eyes. Choking back something that felt treacherously like a sob, he forced a rakish grin. "It was a long time ago. Now I think we were discussing our plans."

She quirked an eyebrow at him. "Is that what you call it?"

He let that finger trace up from her chin to caress her bottom lip and watched with some satisfaction as her lips parted a fraction of an inch. "I didn't have time to prepare any dinner ahead of time. But I would be glad to go grab something from the restaurant kitchen and we can take it upstairs."

She glanced at the ceiling.

"The loft apartment came with the lease on the premises." He grinned. "Pastry chefs do most of our work early in the morning before the restaurant opens, so the line cooks don't deflate all our soufflé's."

The corners of her lips turned upwards

into a grin and she nibbled at his finger playfully. "I would never have guessed that you had a problem with a deflating soufflé."

She wriggled her pelvis slightly against his hips and his cock throbbed.

"See?"

He kissed the naughty grin right off her lips at that, sucking and nibbling until they were both out of breath.

"Hang on," he pulled back with regret. So, so much regret. "I've been thinking about your proposal."

"Oh yeah?" she asked, stepping back in closer. "Me too."

He smiled and took a breath, trying to steel himself. "It will never work."

She raised an eyebrow.

"You said that Rob was in Brazil. As soon as we get Helmut all riled up, he will be here to break us up. Rob will just wait in the jungle for it all to blow over."

She quirked her lips, frowning. "Maybe."

"I have a plan of my own to propose." He leaned back in until their lips were almost touching. "This has to be bigger than just a hot little fling. Way bigger."

She leaned forward, melting against him. "How big?"

"Run away with me to Las Vegas. We will tell them that we are eloping. Marry me, Kelsie."

CHAPTER FOUR

Kelsie took a scalding sip of her mocha, tasting more cream than coffee. It was too hot and too sweet and not nearly wet enough to soothe her dry mouth. But the paper cup was deliciously warm on her fingers, and it gave her something to do. Something besides check her suitcase (zipped and waiting), her phone (no messages), her plane ticket (safely tucked between the pages of the novel in her lap), or the time.

There was over an hour left to wait before she boarded her flight to Las Vegas, and she was already tired of the terminal. Tired of the magazine selection at the snack stand. Tired of the TV monitors playing an endless loop of bad news. Tired of sitting here alone.

He isn't coming.

She checked the time again. Marq should have been here by now. Or her mother should be calling her endlessly to beg her not to elope. Or Helmut should be sweeping in with his private jet to rescue her.

She still couldn't quite believe that she had agreed with Marq's plan. Had agreed to marry him, or at least pretend to. The whole thing took less than 48 hours to put together, including booking the travel and drafting up a pre-nuptial agreement just in case something unforeseeable happened between the chapel and the annulment. Assuming they even got to the altar. Assuming they boarded the plane together.

Kelsie was betting they wouldn't need all that legalese at all. Kelsie had emailed Alice a copy of the pre-nup and their travel itinerary and a quick run-down of the itinerary. Rob got a message also, about the upcoming wedding, but hinting that Helmut knew about her plans. For Helmut and her mother's benefit, she left strategically placed clues.

She fully expected her pre-wedding festivities to be busted up. Rob would call Mom and demand an explanation. Mom would call Helmut. Helmut and Mom would call Alice, who had strict instructions to only divulge the name of the hotel and wedding chapel, and say nothing of the true reason for the wedding. Together, they would follow her trail straight to the Gambling Capital of the World.

If only Marq would follow through on his end of the deal. Assuming he didn't strand her at the airport. Kelsie gulped and tried another small sip of her coffee. Maybe caffeine wasn't the best choice for soothing frayed nerves.

Her phone rang.

"Are you drunk?"

Kelsie grinned at the genuine concern in Alice's voice. "Not a drop. I swear."

"Are you being blackmailed, then? Held at gunpoint? Inhale too much aerosol sunscreen?"

She leaned back as far as she could in the hard little airport chair. "I am of sound mind and body."

"I doubt it. Your plan is crazy enough already, but who's the guy? What happened to the volleyball player? Why didn't you tell me all this was happening?"

"The player turned out to be, well, a player. And I've known Marq since I was a kid, so he's not a stranger. He's like a brother to me. And the last three times I've tried to call you, you were out with your boyfriend."

Silence on the other end. Kelsie could almost picture Alice nibbling on the ends of her long light brown hair. It was one of her nervous habits. "Guilty as charged. Look, I'm sorry about that..."

Kelsie softened her voice. "Hey, no big deal. We all get caught up in our own lives sometimes. I'm not mad. But are you okay with what I sent? Will you help me?"

"I guess. But I don't know if this is going to work the way you think it will."

Just then, she spotted Marq from across the terminal. He had on jeans and a long-sleeved black dress shirt open at the collar, arms crossed over his chest as he scowled at one of the TV monitors. Sexy. Very sexy. He also looked very annoyed at whatever he was reading. She tried to wave at him, but he didn't see her right away. Still, just seeing him made her exhale a little of the pent-up breath she'd been holding all morning.

"Everything will be fine. I know it will."

"Sure, Kels. But isn't it time to quit expecting your brothers to rescue you? You're too old for these kinds of games. Why don't you just hire a therapist?"

Kelsie let out a little harrumph. "I wish things were that easy. I envy you, you know that? You and your family actually like each other. Mine's just different. We're all way to stubborn for that. Hey, I've got to go. Marq is here."

"Ok. Take care, girlfriend. Call me right away if you need anything. And send me a picture. Even if the marriage only lasts a few hours, I still want to see the dress!"

"Deal."

Marq ran fingers through his hair as he scanned the monitor for the gate for his flight. This was the most batshit crazy thing he had done in his life. For a guy who'd done hard time, that was saying something.

Someone jostled his elbow and he stiffened and gritted his teeth, holding his composure together by grit and exhaustion and not much else. The city names on the screen swam together, some blinked, and still he couldn't find Las Vegas.

Damn airports. Damn security guards. Damn Julie.

Julie had made him late. He left his place this morning with plenty of time to stop by Julies with a cookie for her son, little Joaquín, and some money for her. Little Joaquín was his cousin Joaquín's kid. The son his *primo*--his cousin--never had a chance to meet. They'd all gone to high school together--Marq, Joaquín, Julie, and Kelsie's brother Rob. Julie and Joaquín had been *novios*--sweethearts--since Jr High, and Julie got knocked up the night of their senior prom.

Joaquín was a lot like Marq those days. A little rough. A lot wild. So damn young and full of himself. But he loved Julie and in those last weeks before the accident, he had been making plans. He had already started applying for jobs, was talking about joining the union and becoming an electrician. Starting a real career. Growing up.

One fucking party. One stupid car ride. One huge mistake.

Joaquín died at the scene of the car accident, leaving Julie alone and pregnant. Marq swore that he would take care of her, but she had the baby while he was in prison. Little Joaquín was in Kindergarten before Marq met him for the first time. Now that he had his own business, he was finally able to make good on that promise. After years of Julie scraping together a living on welfare and whatever jobs she could take with a kid in tow, he was able to offer her a place as the head bartender at his restaurant. Health insurance. Stability.

And cookies for little Joaquín, who every year looked more and more like his father. Marq made a point of spending time with the boy, doing as much guy stuff as he could think of. Stuff dads did with their sons. Not that Marq's father had ever been that kind of dad.

He made the mistake of telling Julie about his trip with Kelsie, and she flew off the handle. Called Kelsie a whore and a few other choice words. He spent more than an hour calming her back down and re-assuring her that he knew what he was doing.

He had no idea what he was doing here.

Marq blinked again as the screen refreshed and then swore in Spanish as he realized he'd been looking at the Arrivals list instead of Departures.

As if the confrontation with Julie hadn't been so bad, he'd been harassed by airport security. *Randomly selected, my ass.*

The crabby pudgy gate agent who'd checked his ID had taken one look at the tattoo peeking out from the sleeves of Marq's shirt and sent him straight to the side to be frisked and harassed.

"Gate C3"

Kelsie. She wore a short little skirt that showed off long bare legs in a way that stirred something in his cock and a bright-eyed smile that stirred something else in his gut.

He exhaled, and looked her over one more time, enjoying the view. Enjoying the way she blushed just slightly under his gaze.

She hooked an arm in his. "You're late."

He shrugged, slung his bag over one shoulder, and allowed her to steer him through the halls. "Security sucked."

"I was worried that you decided that I was insane and changed your mind."

They stopped in front of a row of chairs to put down their bags. She didn't meet his eyes and he weighed his next words carefully.

"You might be insane. But I haven't changed my mind. I promised to come, so here I am. I always keep my promises."

CHAPTER FIVE

There was simply too much to look at for Kelsie to take in everything. Their cab careened onto Las Vegas Blvd and then squeezed itself into a line of traffic that writhed with the same impatient energy as the crowds that lined the sidewalks. Cars squeezed into impossibly small gaps, but their blinking turn signals were lost on streets illuminated with the dizzying array of neon lights that turned the hot Nevada night into a frenzied rave. Honking horns were drowned by music pumped from six directions at once. The pedestrians staggered in and out of bars and shops and casinos, across skywalks, on and off of trams, wearing tiny dresses that made beach cover-ups look modest, bearing drink cups and cigars and attitudes of carefree independence.

"There are so many people out for a weeknight."

The corner of Marq's mouth turned up, but his eyes focused on something outside his window. "Weekday, weekend. Eleven AM, eleven PM, makes no difference. Vegas never sleeps."

"Do you come here often?"

He didn't answer right away.

Kelsie swallowed, unsure of whether to ask him again. Something in his far-off gaze stopped her, and made her wait.

"I almost took a job here a couple of years ago, opening a restaurant for a celebrity chef."

"That sounds exciting."

He shrugged.

"So you turned down the offer and decided to open your own restaurant instead?"

She waited for his answer, and he was slow to answer again. Like on the plane. She had tried for the first half hour or so to start conversations. About the weather. About his work. About the Dolphins' chances of getting to the Super Bowl. Anything to draw him out. And every question was the same. He answered slowly, with the fewest words he could use. Finally, she had given up and pulled out a book to read. He had smiled at that and closed his eyes for a nap.

"I'm sorry. I talk too much sometimes."

He turned then, his eyes focusing on her as though really seeing her for the first time. "No," he said softly. "Don't apologize. I'm being an ass."

She shook her head and smiled her best flirtatious smile. She was rewarded with a grin that made his eyes sparkle and her core melt.

"I couldn't take the job because my family was in Palm Beach."

Kelsie opened her mouth to protest.

To tell him that she knew his parents were long gone and he had no siblings. She remembered when his grandmother died when he was in high school. How he told her about it one morning at her mother's kitchen counter. How her twelve-year-old self had recognized that pain in his eyes.

That was the day she had decided to love him. She was young, but she knew how it felt when she lost her dad. How it hurt to see other children with their fathers. How she yearned for the scent of Daddy's cologne and the feel of his arms around her, protecting her from the world. How she missed his laughter and his her hand in his and the way he would dance her around the living room and call her his princess.

Teenage Marq had shown her a side of himself that he didn't even share with Rob, and she had hugged that feeling to herself and treasured it. She knew that he hurt, and she also sensed that his revelation was for her ears only.

She closed her mouth instead.

The cab pulled to a stop under the covered portico of an enormous monstrosity of a hotel.

"Welcome to the Bellagio," said the cab driver.

Kelsie looked so beautiful and so vulnerable that it made Marq's cock throb and his heart constrict. He knew he was being a complete ass to her.

He couldn't shake Julie's words from this morning's verbal assault. She had accused him of selling out, of pandering to the rich snobs who ruined his life. Told him that the rich bitch--her words--would destroy him a second time.

Damn if it wasn't true to some degree. The thought had swum through his head all the way to the airport. And all through the flight. It gnawed at his gut and soured all his words. And yet she kept looking at him with something like kindness or affection or worry as she tried to make small talk.

He caught the cab driver giving a slant-eyed look towards the tattoo on his arm as he handed over cash for their trip from the airport and glared at the guy when he made no obvious offer to retrieve their luggage from the trunk.

"I can take mine." Kelsie reached for the handle to her suitcase--a sleek pink one that looked shiny and new.

"I've got this." He flashed her one of those grins he kept for his best customers. "Why don't you watch the fountain show while I go check us in."

She accepted his offer with ease and he watched her head around the walk before hefting his worn old duffel over one shoulder to carry into the lobby.

He glanced around at the acres of marble and sky-high columns and took a deep breath. This time, he was here as a guest, not a hopeful employee. He had every right to stride across to the desk as though he belonged here, and he refused to acknowledge the chill in his palms as he pulled his ID and credit card from his wallet.

He left their luggage with a bellhop and followed the path Kelsie had taken earlier. One of the hotel's famous fountain shows was in progress, with dozens of jets of water dancing in time to a crooning love song. He slid in next to her at the concrete balustrade that edged the expanse of water.

She watched the fountains; he watched her. Her eyes were wide and her lips were parted in half smile, half wonder. The lights of the Strip, garish and bright off in the distance, looked like starlight reflected in her eyes. All too soon, the show was over, and she aimed all that starlight and wonder straight at him.

He was lost.

He couldn't remember the last time he got tongue tied in front of a woman. He spent hours at his restaurant, chatting with the customers, charming the bachelorettes and divorcees and other ladies groups who came for his indulgent drinks and desserts.

But with Kelsie, he opened his mouth and then shut it when he realized he had no idea what to say next.

She scanned the crowds lining the sidewalks and craned her neck around the clusters of other tourists doing the same thing. "I want to go for a walk and see some of the sights. Do you want to come with me?"

Relief washed over him. "Absolutely."

Kelsie and Marq walked in silence for a few blocks. Not that there was a good opportunity for her to say much. The crowds were too thick and the music was too loud and there were too many interesting sights to take in. The fake Eiffel Tower, and the fake Statue of Liberty, the fake castles, the fake Italian manses. Every street corner held actors in costumes--anything from fat bearded men in showgirl outfits to Stormtroopers to Sponge Bob to mimes and musicians. People kept handing her cards advertising different bars or drink specials or shows. She managed to refuse most and discretely toss the rest in a trash can.

She peeked at Marq every now and then, wondering what was going on in his head. He wore a stony, determined look, unfazed by all the glitz around them.

They were approaching yet another casino surrounded by yet another half dozen posh-looking restaurants when he finally spoke up. "Come with me for a minute. I have a friend from cooking school who works here. Let me see if he's around."

He took her hand and she let him lead her to the bar of a sushi-and-ramen restaurant. She glanced at the menu on the way in. Alice would be doubled over laughing at the outrageous prices. Her best friend had practically lived on the stuff when they were in undergrad--the kind that cost a buck for ten packets at the grocery store.

She ordered a glass of wine from the bartender and watched as Marq said something to the hostess, who then disappeared into the back of the restaurant. He had barely sat down next to her when a tall, thin, Asian man burst out of the kitchen area with a fierce scowl etched into his chiseled features.

He wore black striped pants and a white chef's jacket, and clutched a towel in one hand. "Marq. Man, you never said you were coming into town."

"Wei. How have you been?" The two men shook hands and one of them--she couldn't tell which--tugged the other close for that manly chest bump that sometimes passed for a hug.

Beneath one of Wei's rolled up white sleeves, Kelsie caught a glimpse of a black tattoo, similar to Marq's.

"Good. Life is good." Wei took the bar stool on the other side of Marq and the two men launched into some discussion that she could only half catch. It was littered with people and cities. She thought she caught the name of one of her brother Helmut's favorite restaurants from downtown Chicago. She nursed her wine glass and tried not to look like she was eavesdropping. Or impatient.

Wei kept giving her the eye over Marq's shoulder and she smiled at him. Finally Marq seemed to catch on. "Kelsie, this is Wei Zang. He and I went to culinary school together. And Wei, this is Kelsie, my..."

Fiancée. The word felt foreign even inside her own head. Kelsie held out her hand and filled in Marq's blank with the safer answer. "Friend."

Wei smiled and shook her hand. His fingers were long and wiry like the rest of him, and had as many callouses and burn scars as Marq's. "It is my pleasure to meet you, friend of Marq. I hope he hasn't told you a thing about me."

"Nope. Not yet anyway."

"Good." He grinned wider, revealing crooked teeth. "I hope he keeps it that way until after you leave Las Vegas. That way you might like me. How long are you staying?"

"Just a couple of days," said Marq.

"Excellent. Too bad I am working tonight.

Stay and have dinner on me, and maybe we can get together tomorrow."

Marq glanced her way. "Are you hungry?"

They had both eaten something on the plane, and her stomach was tied in a knot. And, with the three-hour time difference from home, she was feeling sleepy. "Not especially. But I don't mind if you would like to stay."

He shook his head. "Rain check, my friend. We should go settle in for the night."

Wei fake-punched Marq in the bicep. "Call me tomorrow and we will go out."

"Deal."

Now that she had realized just how sleepy she was, she couldn't stifle a couple of yawns as they walked back towards the Bellagio.

"How is your plan working?" he asked when they found a rare quiet stretch of pedestrian walkway.

"Um. I guess it's okay. I posted a few pictures to Facebook and Alice is all set with her part. Actually, she might have already tried to call my mom." She pulled her phone out and frowned. No texts, no missed calls, no notifications at all. "But then, it's really late at home."

He nodded. "So, until we hear otherwise, tomorrow we go get our marriage license."

"If we need to."

He punched the elevator button to their floor. Kelsie glanced at her phone again. No bars. Maybe the reception was bad with all of the buildings and so many people in such a small space in one city. Maybe once she got to her room, the messages would begin flooding in.

She followed Marq without really paying attention to her surroundings. He stopped in front of a pair of doors and handed her a plastic room key. "The rooms adjoin, but I thought you might like your own. For when your family arrives."

She accepted the card with another stifled yawn. "Makes sense. I guess."

He leaned in close and kissed her, gently, sweetly on the lips. She leaned in, loving the feel of his mouth on hers, running her hands up his chest. But he pulled back and set her hand gently off of him. His eyes were black and his fingers seemed to tremble just before he let go of her to open the door to his own room. The kiss left her feeling bereft and empty.

"Until tomorrow."

CHAPTER SIX

The flowers she clutched with cold, sweaty palms had plastic stems and lurid pink petals and the air smelled of stale cigarette smoke and day old booze. But the minister, or celebrant, or whatever-his-title-was of the shabby Vegas wedding chapel wore a crisp white shirt beneath a respectably cut suit jacket. He had kind eyes and a pair of champagne flutes bubbling with promise.

"Are you ready, my dears?" He handed Kelsie and Marq each a glass and motioned toward the double doors leading to the altar.

Marq stood by the storefront window on the far side of the waiting room, watching the streams of cars passing through the street, their exhaust adding a hazy quality to the already scorching August evening in the city.

He looked up and caught her gaze. His mouth looked tight around the corners, and the set of his shoulders was stiff. But something in his expression heated as his eyes flicked over her, and Kelsie felt a leap in her belly.

He smiled, and her knees nearly went weak. Nerves, she thought. Nerves and crazy nerve endings.

She felt as shocked as Marq had looked in his office last week when he blurted out the proposal. Her batshit crazy idea had been to stage a fling followed by some dramatic fight that would make her brothers swoop in and rescue her.

"Not enough," Marq had said. "Just a fight won't be enough for Rob. It has to be bigger than that. Marry me."

She didn't think they would actually got through with it. But here they stood.

Marq came over and took Kelsie's hands in his, warming her fingers. "Any word?"

She shook her head. "I just checked my phone. Nothing."

He exhaled, and she wasn't sure whether it was disappointment or relief. "In that case, Kelsie, would you do me the great honor of becoming my wife?"

The romantic words hit her in the gut, and she felt a little warmth kindle inside her.

The ceremony sped by Marq in a cacophony of disjointed sensations. The delicate warmth of Kelsie's hands in his. The choking scent of decaying flowers. The tinny crackle of the prerecorded wedding march. The way, at the moment his eyes locked with hers, his breath caught in his chest and he fell somewhere deep into her eyes. The feather light touch of her lips as they kissed. The way that kiss both rescued him and destroyed him all at once.

He pressed the kiss harder, cupping one hand behind her head and the other around the curve of her lower back, pulling her close. Pulling himself back up from the drowning sensation. Back to the familiar ache of her pelvis against his. Back to the fresh scent of oranges that clung to her hair. Back to the tawdry chapel with its faded carpet and the impatient smile of its minister.

"Congratulations to you both. I wish you a lifetime of marital bliss. Now if you will kindly continue through those doors to your left, my assistant will be happy to arrange for your complimentary photograph and your paperwork."

Kelsie drew back first, away from his hands and his lips, and gave him a bright cool smile. She tucked her arm in his and he allowed her to drag him away from the altar. He must have said the right words and made the right motions, but the only coherent thought in his head was, "Mine. She is mine."

It was more of a visceral feeling than a thought. There was no logic to it. This marriage was as fake as the Eiffel Tower and Statue of

Liberty on the Strip. Just a temporary fairy tale. The ending to this story was already written, and "ever after" wasn't part of it. But he could not shake the words from echoing through his being.

He followed Kelsie into the backseat of a taxi where the length of her legs pressed against his, and he smiled into her glowing eyes.

"Cheers." She handed him an open champagne bottle. "The toasting glasses were loaners, but we paid for the whole bottle."

He accepted it and took a swig, choking lightly as the bubbles hit his throat.

Kelsie laughed. Not one of her self-conscious chuckles or sexy little teasing laughs. This one came from somewhere deep inside and had her bent over, clutching her middle as tears peeked from the corners of her eyes.

He felt a grin splitting the frozen muscles of his face and melting through the fog of the wedding ceremony. "Hey now. What ever happened to 'In sickness and in health'?"

"I vowed to take the good times with the bad, but I never promised not to laugh about it." She took the bottle back and took a slow drink of her own.

Marq watched jealously as her lips caressed the opening of the glass. She set the empty bottle on the floor and he pulled her onto his lap. Her cheeks were flushed and the strands of her hair were beginning to escape the loose bun at the nape of her neck. He brushed one away from her cheek.

"How much of that did you drink?" He asked softly as his fingers traced the line of her cheekbone.

Her lips parted in a soft sigh and she leaned her face against his hand. "Not too much. I promise."

Lust coiled tight and low as she turned to kiss his thumb, flicking it lightly with her tongue. His cock throbbed hard against her butt and she squirmed lightly, teasingly in his lap. "So, does our prenup allow for a wedding night?"

She trailed her teeth lightly on his thumb and he stifled a groan. "Mmm. Yes. Absolutely."

Marq was not clear whether he kissed Kelsie or whether she kissed him. All he knew was that their lips were joined, hot and hungry. Their hands were everywhere. Hers undoing the buttons of his shirt. His weighing a breast, rounding the curves of her hips. They had one breath. They had one need.

If they offended the taxi driver or any of the other hotel guests in the lobby, he didn't care. It was a minor miracle that they reached their hotel room still mostly clothed.

The curve of Kelsie's back with its hints of

bare skin peeping through a sheer, lacy panel that dipped from shoulders to her waistline was by far the sweetest sight Marq had ever seen.

The shimmery white fabric of her dress clung to her hips and thighs, ending at a spot right below her knees that should look modest, but instead called his attention to the curve of her butt and the fact that she didn't seem to be wearing any panties.

He gulped as the hotel door slammed behind, leaving them alone in the quiet of their room. Tall windows on the far wall overlooked the carnival of lights of the strip, their rainbows dappling across the dim room and catching in the wisps of her hair.

She set the empty champagne bottle and her small bouquet on the dresser.

Then she turned.

She slipped off one shoe. Then the other.

A single lock of hair escaped from the clip and drifted down beside her temple, the end curling next to her lips.

Her lips...

His cock throbbed almost painfully, and a hard knot of desire and anticipation and maybe something else curled in his gut.

Her lips were swollen from his kiss in the cab. Her lipstick was long gone. They were parted just slightly, and he watched, mesmerized, as her she wetted them delicately with her tongue.

She smiled, and heat flushed up, enveloping his body in sweet, agonizing flames.

In two swift steps they were eye to eye, their breaths mingling. She smelled of citrus and champagne and flowers.

He brushed that wayward lock backwards, behind her ear, tracing the sway of her earlobe down to the side of her neck.

She shivered and lifted her arms.

He inhaled, waiting for her touch on his chest, his arms, his shoulders.

But instead, she reached behind her head to find the remaining hair clips. The motion lifted her breasts until the tips just brushed his chest through his shirt.

She let her hair fall down around her shoulders, releasing its scent of fruit.

"*Amor mío*, you are beautiful," he whispered into her ear. She shivered again and he nibbled lightly at the sensitive spot behind the lobe.

She let out a soft sound that was half sigh, half growl.

While he traced a line of kisses and gentle nips down her neck to her collar bone, she slid her hands up the front of his chest to work on the buttons of his shirt.

The cool touch of her fingers on his blazing hot flesh sent waves of desire coursing through him.

He wanted her. Naked. Writhing. Soft and sleek beneath him, or maybe above him. He wanted her now. He wanted all of her.

She freed his shirt and he shrugged it off.

He found the hem of her dress and lifted it upwards, hands stroking each inch that he revealed.

Long, sleekly muscled thighs. Then hips. A silky white thong covered the curls at the peak of her legs.

His mouth went dry at the sight.

She raised her arms above her head, and he obliged by pulling the dress up and off.

Her breasts were full with dark pink-brown tips, the tips hard and pointed.

With an impatient sound, she stepped into his arms, pressing those peaks against his chest, and grasping his head with both hands. She pulled him in and kissed him, devouring his lips and tongue the way he had devoured hers earlier.

He was drowning.

He found her hips, so smooth and bare with only the wisp of silk on each side. He traced the back of the thong to where it disappeared at the crevice between her cheeks and was rewarded with an extra gasp as she wriggled even closer, grinding her hips upward against his.

She was the one who turned him, backing him gently until the bed was behind his knees, not breaking their kiss.

His breath was ragged, his heart thundering in his chest. When she slipped hands between their bodies to work the zipper of his slacks, he had to grit his teeth.

Her fingers teased his cock through the layers of pants and boxer shorts, and she tugged at the layers impatiently.

He kicked off his shoes and bent to pull his remaining clothes off. On his way back up, he allowed his fingers to trace Kelsie's waistline and ribcage.

His thumbs found the curve of her breasts and she gasped and leaned subtly back allowing him full access. Her hair streamed down her back in a black satin wave. Her cheeks were flushed with exertion and a hint of stubble burn where he had nibbled the curve of her jawbone. Her eyes were dark pools, heavily lidded and glistening with passion.

He watched those eyes as he flicked thumbs lightly over her nipples. Watched as her pupils darkened even more. Watched as she closed her eyes in pleasure as he cupped her breasts. Watched as she gasped and moaned as he squeezed.

He teased her nipples between his thumb and forefinger and let the sweet sound of her moans send jolts of fire that made his cock jerk in response.

Then he bent to taste her breasts.

She put her hands on his shoulders and gave him a gentle push so that he sat backwards onto the bed. She stepped closer, straddling one of his legs.

His mouth had free access to her breasts, and her pelvis ground lightly against his thigh.

The skin of her belly was soft over lithe muscles.

He found the top of her thong, and then lower.

She was hot and wet and gasped as his fingers found her clit. She tilted her hips against his hand, the movements becoming more and more frantic.

He yanked the fabric down and off of her and pulled her backwards onto the bed. Onto him.

He lay back, helpless as she straddled his thighs. She took his hands from her breasts, capturing them and keeping them still as she studied him.

She touched the black marks of the tattoo that circled his right wrist and crawled up his arm. Then his shoulders. She explored his collar bone, and down his sternum, teasing his own nipples lightly before continuing the heady torture.

His cock was hard and aching against his belly, begging for her touch. She touched his ribs, his belly button, the small puckered scar just above his left hip.

He was paralyzed by her touch, and mesmerized by the sight of her breasts, her belly, the dark folds of her sex parted.

"You are the beautiful one," she whispered. Wandering fingers closed on his cock.

He was lost. Her hands stroked him, squeezing and tugging and cupping.

He was hers. Utterly at her mercy.

He reached for a breast with one hand, his fingers sliding to her clit with the other.

Alternatingly frantic and slow, they brought each other to the brink.

Her touch was almost too much. He knew he would explode in her hands if she didn't stop.

He gently guided her over and onto her back. He found a condom from the pack he had placed in the nightstand drawer. She took it from him and unrolled it onto his length.

Then he was inside her. Their breath came heavy and ragged. They moved as one. They breathed as one. Adjusting, rocking, teasing, circling. He slipped a hand between them to tease her clit again until she came tight and hot, rippling around his cock. He slammed into her again and again, riding the waves of her climax as his built until she was joining him again on the ascent.

Their bodies were slick with sweat and her legs were wrapped around his waist, urging him deeper. Faster. Closer.

His balls contracted as he exploded into her soft, wet, heat as she came around him a second time. She whimpered into his shoulder, kissing his neck and pulling him closer as her own orgasm flowed.

When the waves subsided, he wrapped his arms around her, pulling her close to him while their breathing slowed.

She fit perfectly in his embrace.

CHAPTER SEVEN

Wei's one bedroom apartment reminded Kelsie of the place she shared with Alice--tiny, outdated and utterly lacking in style or character. His furniture was worn and the dining room chairs were mismatched. But the walls echoed with laughter of a dozen of Marq and Wei's friends crammed around the table, and the food he placed in front of them was divine.

She took a bite of salmon crusted with a spice combination that made her tongue sing, dipped in the drizzle of sauce that Wei had dotted around their chipped dinner plates. "If I hadn't seen you cook this myself, I would never have believed that this could come out of a kitchen so small."

Wei shrugged and swigged a gulp of his beer before answering with a completely serious face. "It's isn't the size of a chef's kitchen that matters. It's how he uses the equipment he's got."

Marq snorted and Kelsie nearly choked

on her bite. "In that case, lucky for me, Marq lacks neither size nor skill. In the kitchen."

Under the table, she felt Marq's fingers find the hem of her short dress. He didn't squeeze her leg or try to lift her skirt. Just traced small, delicate circles on her skin.

"I propose a toast to the newlyweds," said Wei, raising his bottle. "A good marriage is like a good cut of steak. It only gets better with age. Keep your lives full of spice, your fire hot, your cream sweet--"

Marq's hand stilled on her thigh and heat warmed Kelsie's cheeks as Wei paused to wait for the laughter at the table to die down.

"May your meringues keep their peaks stiff, and your dough always rise. And may the buns from your oven be plentiful."

Glasses and bottles clinked all around. She forced a smile to her face and took a sip of her wine. It didn't help her suddenly dry mouth, or the knot in her stomach. She turned and found Marq studying her with guarded eyes and she wondered what he was thinking. Would he regret not telling Wei the truth about their marriage? Would his friend feel betrayed when he realized that the adorably heartfelt and risqué toast was all for nothing?

Knives clinked on glasses, and she blushed again, realizing that the rest of the table was begging the two of them to kiss. *Just like a real wedding reception, only smaller*. The thought only made her feel worse. Marq's lips pressed to hers, and she returned the kiss, but her heart wasn't in it. Neither was her libido. She whispered to him "I need to step outside for a minute for some fresh air."

He nodded and helped pull her chair out for her to stand, much to the amusement of the other guys at the table. A few catcalls and a whistle or two followed them as the stepped out the sliding glass doors onto a tiny balcony that overlooked the parking lot.

The night was still warm with the residual heat of the day, but dry. So much drier than home. She missed the tang of salty ocean air. They quietly together at the railing for several long heartbeats. "You have good friends here."

He shrugged. "Yeah. I've been so busy lately with my restaurant, I forgot how much I missed these guys."

"Why did you leave?"

"It's a great place for a culinary career. Right up there with New York City as a place that can make or break a chef. That's why Wei stays. And the rest of them. That, and the easy life. Casinos, drugs, women. The life sucks you in and doesn't let go easily."

She didn't have a response to that.

"I had a job opportunity with a big-name celebrity chef opening a high-end restaurant in one of the casinos. But the offer came with strings attached. He knew about my past, about my record. Figured I'd be willing to take care of a few side deals for him."

She sucked in her breath as she realized what he had gone through. Blackmail.

"I refused. They kicked me out of the hotel room they'd given me. Dropped me and my stuff on the street, barely an hour after I said 'no'. If I stayed, that was the best I could expect. That everyone would use my past against me. So I came home."

"And it was better in Palm Beach? Wouldn't you have just as hard of a time with your record?"

His lips quirked in an ironic smirk. "Back home, a Latino like me is expected to have a rap sheet. No one there ever expected me to want a better life. It didn't even phase the bankers when I went to apply for a loan to open the restaurant. They made it harder on me, sure. I had to have more savings, worse interest rates, more insurance. Shocked the hell out of the loan officer when he saw what I'd built with his money. He was expecting walls covered in fake Mexican murals and a menu full of tacos and margaritas."

She sat in silence for a few moments watching an over-sized pickup truck trying to turn around in the narrow end of the street by the dumpster.

"My turn to ask you questions. Why do you care so much about getting your brothers to talk to each other?"

She drained the last few drops of wine from her glass before answering. "We are family. Family is supposed to take care of each other, right?"

He shrugged.

"That, and this feud between Rob and Helmut has gone on long enough. They both need to grow up. Whatever stupid fight they had was twelve years ago. I don't care what the argument was about. I just think it's time to forgive and forget."

He shifted his stance a little. Stiffened a little. Pulled away a little. Kelsie felt that little movement like a vast canyon stretching between them.

When he spoke, his voice was soft, almost too soft. "This is all about you, isn't it."

She inhaled, weighing her words before she spoke. Forming her argument, choosing her phrasing. "When Dad died, Mom sort of disappeared into her grief. So, Helmut, Rob and I promised each other that we would always take care of each other. They are the only family I have, and it kills me that I can barely mention their names without someone getting mad. Or worse, they just disappear for months at a time. I feel like I am losing them both a little more every day.

"So, if that makes this all about me, then yes. It is all about me. I want my family to be around. I want to be able to depend on them. I want things to be like they used to be."

He opened his mouth and then shut it and looked away. She could feel the canyon between them, growing deeper and colder with every breath, but she didn't know why. She shivered suddenly and rubbed her arms to warm them.

He looked at her and his gaze softened. He draped a steady, warm arm around her shoulders and pulled her in tight. It felt right, there, in his arms.

"Some families you are born into. And some you choose."

She leaned her head on his chest, trying to swallow the lump that refused to leave her throat. "So why can't I choose the one I was born into?"

The ringtone of Marq's cell phone cut through the quiet night. He pulled away from her, yanked it out of his pocket, and scowled.

"Who is it?"

He ignored her question and turned away, answering in a rapid Spanish that her paltry vocabulary had no hope of catching. She could see the muscles of his shoulders and neck tense up, and the tone of his voice sounded harassed and hurried.

Whatever that was about, she wasn't part of it.

She smoothed her hair down and plastered on a smile and stepped back inside, rejoining the table where her dinner and her wine waited.

The conversation and laughter swirled over her head while she finished the rest of her salmon and some kind of roasted potato dish that was equally divine.

As she was draining the last of her wine, Wei disappeared into the kitchen and rummaged in his tiny fridge. He emerged a minute later with a white bakery box and a wide grin, then ceremoniously cleared a space in the middle of the table.

She heard the squeak of the sliding door opening behind them, and then Marq was standing over her, one hand on her shoulder.

"Ahem, about time you came back to your party," said Wei. "It's cake time."

"Wei--"

"I am sorry, my dearest Kelsie, that my delicacies cannot possibly equal that of your husband's. So I called in a favor from a friend of mine. He's the head pastry chef at Mandalay Bay--and before you ask, Marq, no you don't know him. He smells like cheese and runs around cursing the staff in French. But his *Charlotte Royale* is award winning."

Wei opened the box with a few flicks of his fingers, letting the cardboard flop open, revealing a dome shaped cake. The sweet scent of chocolate and whipped cream made Kelsie's mouth water.

"I have to go," said Marq as he waved away a knife and spatula that Wei tried to press at him.

Wei's face froze in its grin. "What is it?"

Marq's face looked pale with a slight flush around the temples. "My nephew, Joaquín, is hurt. I have to leave."

Kelsie felt helpless next to Marq's restless energy. He held his fists clenched throughout the cab ride back to their hotel, and sliced his way through the crowded lobby. She all but ran to keep pace with him.

It would have been easier to let him go ahead. He barely acknowledged her presence, and didn't slow to wait for her to slip off her high-heeled sandals. When they reached their joined rooms, the bed had been turned down by housekeeping, with a mint on the pillows, but the door between the two rooms was closed and locked again.

Without a complaint, she stepped back into the hall and entered through her own door. She sank down onto her own bed and contemplated the adjoining door. Beyond it, she couldn't hear any sound though she knew Marq would be packing a suitcase, calling the airline to change his flight home. Preparing to go.

The wine she had downed at dinner made

her feel flushed and light headed, but that was little inconvenience next to the hard knot that formed in her gut.

When had she fallen for the illusion that she herself had designed? Somewhere between the glittering lights and the fake romance of Las Vegas, she forgot that the weekend was a sham. The laughter, the sex...none of it was any more real than the Eiffel Tower or the Statue of Liberty on the Strip. They were always planning to go back home, to reveal the subterfuge. Just not to-night. Not like this.

She poured a glass of water from the bathroom sink and then smoothed her hair. Eye-liner and mascara had smudged below her eyes, giving her that partied-hard-enough-to-regret-it look. With a grimace, she grabbed for a wash-cloth and scrubbed her face clean, then changed into yoga capris and a T-shirt.

Marq didn't glance up when she opened the door. His attention was taken by stuffing clothing haplessly into his duffel bag.

"Do you need a hand?"

That earned her only a sideways look and he brushed past into the bathroom. While he gathered his things from the sink, she tucked in a sweatshirt that was sticking out of his bag blocking the zipper. She spotted one of his shoes hiding under the bed skirt. Right where he had kicked it off last night, followed by his pants and...

And she quietly retrieved it and tucked it inside the bag without a word.

He took the bag gently from her and stuffed a jumble off toiletries and charging cables in without ceremony, then yanked the zipper shut.

His eyes scanned the room like a man expecting an ambush.

"You changed your flight?" she asked.

He sat down heavily next to her on the bed, put his elbows on his knees and dropped his forehead to his palms.

Tentatively, she reached out to touch his shoulder. He didn't pull away at her touch, so she left it there, lightly tracing circles onto the stress-stiffened muscles of his back.

"Thank you." The words were soft, hoarse. They sounded as though he'd spent hours crying, though she had yet to see a single tear.

"For what? I haven't done anything."

He crossed his hand up to cover hers. "For still sitting here."

She turned her hand over and laced her fingers through his icy ones. "What happened to him?"

"He got in a fight at school. The other kid knocked him unconscious. He's in the hospital."

"Is he going to be okay?" She winced even as she asked the question.

"I don't know. Julie--his mom--wasn't

making a lot of sense." He let go of her and ran his fingers through his hair. "I have to go. I was able to get the last seat on the midnight flight. I should be on the road already."

She put a hand on his arm as he went to shoulder his bag, then leaned in close. She threw her arms around his neck for a quick hug.

His cheek was rough next to hers, and his scent and heat surrounded her. She wished she could smooth some of that tension away, or hold his hand. She wished she could go with him. Instead she dropped her arms to let him go.

He leaned down and kissed her. Fiercely. Hungrily. He stole her breath and then abruptly stepped back and headed for the door.

Kelsie gathered her breath with a gulp. "Give me a call when you find out how he's doing. Please?"

"I will."

And then he was gone.

CHAPTER EIGHT

It was dark and drizzling when Kelsie pulled into her mother's driveway. The quiet street where she'd grown up lay cloaked in an eerie, silent fog. After the constant light and roar of the Las Vegas Strip, the familiar scene was surreal in its peacefulness.

Just like how she felt inside. Dark. Bleak. She felt the lack of excitement and the lack of company like a void. One she wasn't sure how to fill.

She had intended to fill the night in Vegas before her flight home with a list of activities she had wanted to try: a spa treatment, a little gambling, maybe a show. There were simply too many options on the spa menu, from massages to facials to wraps and hot stones and some that she couldn't quite understand. The list was overwhelming so she wandered down to the casino and bored herself silly losing a few dollars in slot machines before giving in to a headache from the constant smoke-and-incense smell. She never even looked at show ticket prices, but spent the rest of the night curled up in her bed watching movies on TV.

She even texted Marq. Just once. A super-quick message hoping he'd had a good flight and that his nephew was doing okay. Nothing too needy, too clingy. But he hadn't replied.

She hit the button on the garage door opener with cold, trembling fingers. Mom's car was gone. No one was home.

Kelsie let out the breath she didn't realize she had been holding.

She left her suitcase next to the laundry area in the garage, kicked her shoes off into a stack of flip flops--all hers--by the door, flipping on light switches as she walked into the house.

On the kitchen counter sat a stack of mail and newspapers still in their plastic wrappers. Next to that, a note with written instructions addressed to their next door neighbor about feeding the cat. Her mother had left town for the weekend with her bunco night friends, without so much as a word.

In the stack of mail, a small silver envelope caught her eye. The wedding announcement she had left for her mother to find. Unopened. Buried in a pile of magazines and unopened junkmail. Kelsie snatched it out of the pile. Mom had never even seen it. She didn't know about the trip to Las Vegas. Didn't know about Marq.

A mixture of relief and anger hit her in the gut and she sat down heavily on one of the breakfast counter stools.

Alice had been right. The whole thing was a dumb idea. No one got mad. No one busted up the wedding. No one had paid her any attention at all.

She gulped down a sob that threatened to close up her throat. No use crying, either. There was no one here to soothe her tears. She didn't know how long she sat there, wallowing in her own loneliness before her phone beeped.

It was a text from Marq. "Are you home? Can I see you?"

He found her in the hospital lobby staring blankly at one of the TV screens and fiddling with the ring on her left hand. It was too big for her, but he had been guessing about the right size. She had offered him a ring she already owned to use in the ceremony--something inexpensive and overdone looking, like women wore out with their friends. He had managed to surprise her with this one. No diamonds or anything pricey. Just a white gold band with a delicate carved pattern with tiny flowers engraved on it and an aquamarine, her birthstone. Something she could keep to remember him by. Later.

Kelsie looked anxious and tired. With a

pang, he realized that she couldn't have been home long when he called. If she had taken their original flight home, she'd been up since the break of dawn. Traveling, alone.

That was his fault.

He stopped just short as she spotted him. Her smile wavered, but warmed him anyway.

Damn, but he had missed that smile the past day and a half.

They both spoke at once.

--"How is he?"

--"How was your flight?"

She shook her head. "Your nephew is way more important than my day."

"The doctors say that he will be okay. He has a concussion, but they think he will be able to go home tomorrow." And the juvenile court wanted to see him the day after that. But Marq didn't feel have the energy to explain all of that just yet.

She took a small step forward and brushed something off his temple. Such a small touch.

To hell with the nurses and the reception-ist and everyone else in the waiting room who could be watching. He pulled her to him and kissed her. She wrapped her arms around his neck and kissed him back.

She tasted like chocolate and cinnamon and home.

He rested his forehead on hers, savoring

the feel of her in his arms. "Do you want to meet him?"

"Absolutely."

Her head was still reeling from that kiss as Marq led her down the pediatric wing, where the halls were painted with dancing teddy bears and soccer balls and purple castles. They knocked softly on the door to a patient room, and he stuck his head in.

His nephew was propped up in bed, watching TV.

"Yo, Jo." Spoken with the Spanish J, it sounded like yo-yo.

Joaquín shrugged. "Hey, Tío."

"I have someone I want you to meet." Marq said, frowning.

"Not another doctor, I hope."

Marq grabbed the remote control off the side table and turned down the volume. He waved Kelsie in to his side. "No, she's not a doctor."

She smiled brightly and stuck out her hand. "It's nice to meet you, Joaquín. I'm Kelsie."

Joaquín scrunched up his face and gave Marq a funny look while he shook her hand. "Uh, hi. Call me Jo. Everyone else does. If you aren't a doctor, are you a social worker or something?"

"Nope. Just a friend."

Jo shrugged and grabbed for the remote. "That's what they all say."

Marq gave him a friendly punch on the shoulder. "Mind your manners."

She looked around the room, grasping for something she could relate to. Two brothers, but they were both so much older than she was. She had no idea what a kid this age cared about. "What are you watching?"

"Some dumb show. All they have are kids' shows. Do you want to play a game? They brought me a Wii, but there is only one game. It's no fun to race cars when there's no one to race against."

"Um, sure." She took the controller he handed her and perched on the edge of his bed as he fired up the game.

She was out of practice at video games. Way out of practice.

By the fourth race--four races where Kelsie lost by a comically huge margin--Marq was laughing at her. By the eighth, her hands were cramping and her thumbs throbbing from all her frantic button mashing, but she had at least managed to lose by a much smaller margin.

"Do you want a turn?" she offered him the controller.

Marq smirked and proceeded to beat his nephew soundly for three races in a row.

"Hey, Tío, can I come stay with you this weekend? Did you know he has over *two hundred* channels?" Joaquín's eyes rounded like a starving man facing a donut shop as he spoke.

Marq crossed his arms over his chest and glowered. "You will have to take that up with your mother."

Jo's face fell. "*Mama* said I was grounded for life. But she might change her mind if *you* ask her. Please?"

The door opened and a woman bustled in, followed by a nurse in scrubs. "Ask me what?"

The woman was a few inches shorter than Kelsie and curvy, wearing leggings that clung to a round backside and a lose tank top with a plunging neckline. She was pretty with big black eyes, deeply bronzed skin, and bright lipstick that would have looked jarring on women with less naturally vibrant color. Joaquín's mother was the bartender from Chocolate, Chocolate, Kelsie realized with a start. She felt foolish for not making the connection before.

"Can I go visit Tío Marq this weekend, Mama?"

Julie. Her name was Julie. And she replied to her son's half whine with a short diatribe in Spanish that Kelsie couldn't quite understand. The answer was clearly no, because the boy wilted back onto his pillows and set his jaw in almost a perfect imitation of his uncle. She kept her own mouth shut, feeling awkward to be witnessing the family squabble.

"Excuse me, folks. Visiting hours are over. Only immediate family in the patient rooms after eight," said the nurse.

Julie waved the woman off. "Marq is as close to a father as my son has."

Kelsie felt the exact moment that Julie noticed her. The air in the room seemed to freeze over first, then explode.

"What is *she* doing here?"

Marq took half a step forward, putting his body directly between the two women.

"Mama, this is Marq's friend Kelly. She's fun. But she stinks at Mario Kart." Joaquín looked back and forth between all the adults, clearly confused.

"Kelsie," corrected Marq quietly.

"I know who she is." Julie's voice lowered to something like a growl. "What I don't understand is why you would bring her anywhere near my son."

The words felt like poisoned arrows aimed directly at Kelsie.

"Folks, can you please take this conversation into the hallway? I need to take Jo's vitals now."

Kelsie nudged Marq on the shoulder so that he might let her past. "I can wait outside."

He didn't budge. "It's all right, Julie. We were just hanging out. Keeping him entertained."

Julie's eyes narrowed and her face scrunched up. He fists were balled and she charged toward Marq and Kelsie. "Get out! Get out! Get that *puta* away from my baby."

Kelsie recoiled at the word. *Puta*. Whore. Bitch. "I don't know what you mean--"

"Your brother murdered my *novio*. I don't want you anywhere near my baby." Julie lurched forward, swinging fists wildly toward her.

Ice seized Kelsie's gut at double-punch of words and physical assault.

Marq grabbed Julie by the shoulders and held her back, and Kelsie shot past Marq and into the hallway. She heard him call out her name as she escaped to relative safety. She heard a string of curses in Spanish follow her.

She nearly ran into a security guard near the nurses' station, hurrying toward Joaquín's room. She stopped there, not knowing what to do next.

So cold. She shivered and rubbed her arms trying to warm up.

"Were you just in that room?" asked a man in scrubs from behind the desk. A nurse, or orderly, or doctor, or something. She wasn't sure what he was.

"Yes. Jo's mother just, like, attacked my...Marq. She was screaming at me. I don't even know what happened. I've only met her twice. But she acted like she hated me."

The man shrugged. "People get stressed out in hospitals. And that lady has been pretty high strung with all the cops in and out."

"Cops?" Kelsie glanced back towards Jo's room.

"Why don't wait in the lobby."

She sat on the hard vinyl for what seemed like hours. Every time the automatic doors that led to ward opened, she looked up, hoping to see Marq. But it never was. Finally a hospital security guard came walking through, and made a beeline for her.

"Mrs. Castillo?"

She blinked for half a breath, not quite realizing that he was addressing her. But there was no one else. *Mrs. Castillo.* "Y-yes?"

"Your husband asked me to give you this." He handed her a key. "He said he would see you later at home. Ms. Alvarez is overwrought and talking to one of our family therapists right now. He said he wanted to stay with the boy until his mother calmed down. Said he would take a cab home later."

It was a house key. *His house key.* "Um, thanks."

"Good evening, ma'am."

She closed her fingers over the cool metal while the guard's words replayed in her mind.

Mrs. Castillo. Your husband. *Home.*

CHAPTER NINE

Photos of Joaquín outnumbered pieces of furniture by a large margin in Marq's apartment. Not that it was a fair contest. He had just enough utilitarian pieces for a simple bachelor's life: bed, nightstand but no dresser, couch, TV, coffee table, and three barstools pushed up against a narrow high countertop that must serve as the dining table. Framed photos of the kid lined the shelves of the TV stand, and unframed snapshots covered the front of a smallish refrigerator.

She was surprised that the kitchen was so Spartan. It had a basic range, microwave, fridge, some lower cabinets but no uppers. But with a whole restaurant at his disposal just downstairs from the loft, maybe he didn't need much. One long wall was exposed brick, and high deep-set windows lined another wall overlooking the street. The bathroom had that modern industrial feel with more exposed brick and a thoroughly masculine lack of storage for toiletries.

She liked it. It wasn't fussy; it wasn't

crowded with knickknacks. Just with Marq's obvious adoration of his nephew.

She studied the snapshots on the fridge for a long time, feeling both curious and guilty at the same time, like she was snooping through a medicine cabinet. This felt way more personal.

There were shots of just the boy at different ages, of Marq the kid together, at Disney World and the beach, wearing birthday party hats or carrying fishing poles. But the ones that she couldn't stop looking at, the photos that made her heart knot and her throat tighten, were the pictures of Marq, Joaquín, and Julie together. Holidays, birthdays, outings. They looked like the perfect family.

In one shot in particular, Marq and Julie were dancing in what could have been a wedding or *quinceañera*, with Joaquín clutched to their legs. Marq was laughing down at Jo with that relaxed wide grin that Kelsie had come to crave. But Julie wasn't looking at her son. She was smiling at Marq with a blissfully happy expression, her fingers lightly perched on his shoulder.

She sank down onto the couch, her head spinning.

"Your brother murdered my novio."

She tried dialing Rob first. No answer.

Then Helmut.

He picked up. "Do you have any idea what time it is?"

"I. Um. Well, no, I guess I don't."

He sighed audibly. "I'm in London for a meeting. It's nearly dawn here. I was already up late working on the presentation and had finally fallen asleep."

"Oh. I'm sorry. I have a question."

"One that couldn't have waited for daylight?"

She shifted on the couch. "I said I was sorry, Helmut. How was I supposed to know you weren't home? Did Claire come with you? How long ago did you leave?"

"I've been here since last week. Yes, we both came. She's taking the train through the Chunnel tomorrow to Paris to meet with some airline customers there. Don't you ever talk to mom? "

Kelsie gritted her teeth. "No, apparently not. She's out of town too. I didn't realize she was leaving either."

"Well, since I'm up, you may as well ask. What is all this about."

Here goes. "So I ran into an old friend of the Rob's recently. Do you remember Marq Castillo?"

Silence.

"That was a dumb question. Of course you'd remember him. What happened with him and Rob and their friend Joaquín?"

Helmut's voice was practically a growl. "Damnit, Kelsie, why are you bringing this up now?"

"I, well, I was told by..." She stumbled over the words, not sure how much to say. How to explain. "Told by Julie Alvarez. I don't know if you know her. She knew Joaquín. Was his girl-friend back then, I guess. Anyway, she accused Rob--"

"Don't." He cut her off. "I know who Julie Alvarez is. She used to make threatening phone calls after the accident. She blamed Rob for the whole tragedy. I wanted to feel sorry for her at first, but talking just made her more hysterical."

"What happened? I don't even know the story. Rob would never talk about it."

She heard a sound that was suspiciously like a snort. "Rob won't talk to anyone about an-ything. Not even to the therapist we sent him to. And now he's gone and hidden himself out in the jungle. Like that's going to solve anything. Here's a little advice, Kelsie. You can't run away from your problems."

"Like you did when your affair with Claire hit the Paris tabloids?"

"That was totally different. I didn't hide. I just re-grouped for a while after that, to give her space to get away from all the scandal. I was in love with her and didn't want to destroy her ca-reer by hanging around. That's not the same as cutting off communication with your entire fam-ily and skipping the country."

She tucked her knees up and wrapped her

arms around them. It was late, and she was tired and shivering. "Okay. So, what did happen to Rob that made him run away? I'm not twelve anymore. You can tell me the truth."

"He was running with a bad crowd. With Marq and Joaquín, and a few others. At first it was just a little marijuana. Not that any drug is good, but a lot of kids try that one and don't get in too much trouble. But I think things were way worse than just a little pot. From what I can gather, some kids were dealing, and not just in pot, and they dragged Rob into it. Rob and I fought about that a lot."

"I remember the fights," Kelsie half-whispered.

"I didn't know what to do. I was his brother, not his father." Helmut's voice cracked. "So I was being an overbearing asshole and Rob was being a moody teenager and we butted heads. The next thing I know, he and his low-life friends went on some kind of binge, decided to take Marq's grandmother's car on a joy ride, and got in a car accident. The one kid died at the scene. The other one, Marq, was driving. He got banged up a little. But they took him to the hospital. Rob was the only one who wasn't hurt at all, by some miracle. Like I said, it was just a stupid tragedy. Angry teenage boys doing stupid shit."

She sat there, trying to match Helmut's words with the bits Marq had said. "Marq went to the hospital. So they knew he was doing drugs?"

"I guess so. He was charged with involuntary manslaughter and possession."

"Wait a minute, why does Julie Alvarez hate Rob so much if Marq was driving the car that killed her boyfriend?"

She heard a huff. "I could never get a straight answer out of her. She was really messed up over her boyfriend's death. Like I said, she was always hysterical. I suspect she blamed Rob because nothing happened to him. He didn't get hurt, he didn't get arrested. She blamed him for being lucky."

Her heart constricted, picturing an eighteen year old girl, alone and grieving. Her boyfriend dead, his cousin in jail, and the rich white friend who walked away unharmed. "I bet the hormones didn't help, either."

"What do you mean?"

"She was pregnant," she said flatly. "With Joaquín's baby. She had a little boy, and named him after the dead father."

"Hmm," was all he said for a long time. "I didn't realize she was pregnant, too. That might be what all the hysterics were about. Poor kid. I hope she managed to turn her life around and get out of that mess. Get away from the likes of Marq Castillo so he doesn't drag her and the baby down the same path he was on."

Kelsie looked around the apartment, with

its comfortable furniture and smiling baby pictures. She thought of the restaurant downstairs. The upbeat vibe. The rave reviews it had been getting. She thought of Marq and the way he hooked a tattooed arm around her waist to pull her close and the way he would keep her wine filled but only sip at his own. This was the path that Helmut was so afraid of?

"Helmut?"

"Yeah?"

You're wrong. Marq is way better than all that. You never gave him the chance. But she didn't say any of that. "If you see what looks like a card from me in the mail when you get home, throw it away. Don't even open it. It was a bad prank that one of my friends was playing. So just ignore it. Ignore the whole thing."

The closer Marq got to home, the more his spirits lifted. Kelsie would be there waiting for him.

The sky was already brightening to a pale gray, with a few pink rays setting puffy clouds aglow over the ocean. His insides felt like sand. Coarse, gritty, irritated. He'd spent the night in a fake leather armchair next to Joaquín's bed, too tense to really sleep. One of the staff doctors had prescribed Julie a sleeping pill, and they had sent her to an empty patient room to sleep off her hysteria. He envied her that chance at peace, but had no intention of begging for drugs.

He was not an addict. Never had been. Had barely experimented with anything even before the car accident in high school. And with his rap sheet, it was a chance he would never take. No single night's sleep was worth the kind of harm to his life and career if someone accused him of using.

The past couple of years, work had been his escape from the nightmare of his past. Work and little Jo. He had poured his energy into the food, finding and training the perfect staff, into proving his worth. And he poured his money and his free time into giving Jo the kind of childhood that Marq had always wanted. One with adults around who cared, who modeled good behavior, who made him laugh and learn and think.

He thought he had everything he wanted in life. Right up until Kelsie walked back into it, and showed him the piece that was still missing.

Marq took the steps to his loft two at a time, picturing her sleeping in his bed. Imagining curling his arms around those sweet curves, kissing the back of her neck, feeling her shiver.

She was wide awake and wearing the same dress she had worn to Wei's. He felt the coil of tension inside and exhaustion start to unwind. He exhaled and smiled.

"Hey, gorgeous."

She didn't meet his eyes right away, but focused on her suitcase, on tugging the zipper. Closed.

He glanced at his watch and realized just how long she must have been sitting here alone. "I am sorry about last night."

She smiled up at him finally. But the smile didn't quite light her eyes. She didn't look mad. Just distant. Closed off. "Are your nephew and his mother doing okay?"

The question was polite, without a hint of frostiness. Kind, even. But still he felt the wall between them go up and gulped, his throat tightening as he grasped for a response. "Yes. Everyone's fine. I didn't realize that Julie would go off the deep end like that last night. It wasn't your fault."

"I know. I understand." She hefted the bag onto her shoulder.

"You don't have to go." *Please don't go.*

She hesitated for a breath, and her mouth twitched like she was biting back a grimace. "Actually, I do. Classes start in a couple of days and I need to get to campus. Buy books, supplies. All of that. Two semesters left, then I study for the bar exam. And look for a job. They say the market for lawyers is pretty good in Miami, but there are a lot of us graduating too. Stiff competition. I have a lot of work to do the next few months."

His stomach lurched as though the floor

had dropped out from below him. She was leaving. His feet felt frozen as he watched her move around him. Gracefully, quietly towards the door.

At the door, she turned halfway, talking over one shoulder. "I am sorry I put you through all that drama last night. I talked to my brother after I left. If had known the truth about Julie, and Rob and Joaquín and...well, if I had known I never would have gone. I am sorry I dragged you through my craziness the last week. I..."

Every word felt like a needle to his gut, and the crack in her voice as she trailed off twisted inside him. She knew all about him. She was leaving him.

Her scent still lingered in the air. Her hand was on the door knob. "I will send the paperwork as soon as I get home...for the divorce...Take care, Marq. Good luck with your restaurant. And take care of your family."

CHAPTER TEN

"Get dressed. You're going out with me. We have plans and you aren't weaseling out of it this time."

Kelsie blinked, trying to drag herself awake. "Quit shaking me, Alice."

Alice gave her arm another tug. "Get up off the couch, sleeping beauty. It's seven o'clock in the evening. If I didn't know you better, I would think you started partying without me, the way you passed out."

A few last rays of sunshine crept around the cracks in the mini-blinds, painting the far side of the living room wall with orange and black stripes. Her environmental law textbook had dropped off her lap, crushing half the pages where they smashed into floor, and her highlighter was nowhere to be found. Kelsie sat up a little too quickly and stars danced in front of her eyes. "I was just studying. I have an exam this week."

Alice crossed her arms over her chest and

frowned. She was dressed to go out in white skinny jeans, a silky tank top and high-heeled strappy sandals. "Is that what you call it when you snore on the couch for over two hours?"

Kelsie took a deep breath and stood up, happy that the temporary dizziness had receded. She picked up her book and smoothed the pages as best she could, then stacked another textbook on top to flatten it back out. With any luck, there was no permanent damage. "I guess I was tired. I did go for a run this morning."

That had been the first real exercise in more than two weeks, outside of walking around campus. She was just so wiped every night after classes were done, and her group project meeting for corporate law, and her part time job for the tutoring company. That was only five or six hours a week, but still. It added up.

"I will go change."

She stared at the contents of her closet for as long as she dared, hoping the perfect outfit would jump of the hanger and into her arms. Tonight was supposed to be a celebration of sin-glehood--hers and Alice's. Their summer ro-mances had both faded away once classes got back into full swing. Though maybe drawing up divorce papers wasn't exactly "fading"

After leaving Marq's apartment, she had driven woodenly back to Mom's house. Without stopping to shower or really pack, she stuffed the backseat of her car with her clothes, shoes, the few books she had brought from her own apartment. Most of her toiletries were already packed from the trip, and most of the rest of her belongings were at her apartment down in Miami.

She managed to keep the tears in through the nearly two hour drive, and until after she had hauled all of her things inside and shut herself into her own bedroom. As the semester started up, she was too busy to stare at her phone hoping for a message. But as the days dragged on and she settled into a routine, she found more and more time to contemplate what happened.

Walking around campus, or around town, she would hear a few words of that local Hispanic drawl that reminded her of Marq. She caught a whiff of baking brownies wafting from a local bakery one afternoon and couldn't resist stopping in to buy one. But after a few bites, memories of laughing with him at the bar in his restaurant choked her up and the brownie--not even half as good as his--tasted bitter. She tossed the rest in the trash. That afternoon she finally gathered the divorce papers that she owed him.

Since nothing in her closet really appealed, she went with the least offensive thing she could find. A plain black A-line knit sundress that wasn't too clingy, wasn't too revealing, wasn't too much of anything really. She grabbed a long beaded necklace and earrings to dress it up and put on some lipstick, more to appease Alice than anything else.

Alice had dumped her own guy right after classes started. But unlike Kelsie, her newly single status seemed to have energized her.

The downtown dance club was on the top floor of a 50 story hotel. Poolside. Kelsie followed Alice through the throbbing dancers to the bar and tried to swallow a grimace as her best friend ordered two martinis. The cab that had brought them here had smelled awful, but rolling down the windows in the slow-moving congested traffic was worse. She felt queasy from the all the fumes.

Before their drinks even arrived, two guys appeared, both wearing white button down shirts untucked over jeans, elbows rolled up and top two buttons undone. One of them gave Kelsie's cleavage a once over that lasted far too long. The other smiled at Alice. "Can you settle a bet for us?"

Kelsie's stomach sank. The first guy to talk was always the wingman, and he always approached the friend of the target. That meant that she was the target.

Alice made a show of fishing the olive out of her martini and eating it before smiling broadly. "Try me."

It was all Kelsie could do not to elbow her friend in the ribs. Not only was Alice well aware of the setup, she was going to clear the way for his buddy to talk to Kelsie.

Neither man was bad looking. They both had neatly groomed and styled hair, decently athletic builds, tans that just bordered on fake. One had a more square jaw, but the other had pretty pale blue eyes and perfectly even white teeth that both contrasted with his spray tan.

Wingman grinned. "It's about a cocktail. My buddy Devin here," he slapped his pal on the back. "Was telling me about Ernest Hemmingway's favorite drink. Death in the Afternoon."

Kelsie picked up her glass and held it to her lips. Not quite drinking, just tasting the vodka and vermouth lightly with her tongue. Devin watched her mouth intently and she had to suppress a sigh of annoyance.

"Absinthe," said Alice. "Served in a champagne flute."

Devin leaned in close to Kelsie's ear. "I'm sorry, I didn't catch your name."

She took a full sip. And immediately regretted it.

The room was too smoky. The music too loud. The cab ride. The nap. The ever present malaise.

The bitter alcohol burned her tongue and made her gag. "Excuse me," she tried to get up. Looked frantically for the ladies room.

Then she puked all over Devin and his wingman's shoes.

"You should have told me you were actually sick. We could have postponed this to next week."

Kelsie could only manage a quick "hmmph" before another round of nausea hit her. Alice held her hair back as she knelt over the ladies room toilet, puking up the remains of her lunch. Her stomach had felt so sour lately that she had only picked at her food most days. This morning had been that burst of energy, the jog, a chicken salad at her favorite cafe. Apparently none of the lettuce had actually digested in the eight hours since then.

Finally, the worst was over and she rinsed her face off with cold water in the sink, with Alice hovering like a mother hen.

"I'm not sick, Alice. I'm pregnant."

Outside the bathroom, heavy bass pounded out a heady rhythm. Inside, the silence hung heavier than the thick humidity and smog.

"Let's go home."

Sitting in yet another cab--one that didn't smell so bad, thankfully--Kelsie talked. "I guess I don't know for sure. I haven't bought a test or anything. But I've got all the signs. Nausea, sleeping all the time, my boobs hurt and I feel bloated. I feel like I've got the worst case of PMS ever, but it's been two months since my last period."

Alice slipped her arm around Kelsie's bare shoulders and pulled her close and spoke softly. "I'm so sorry, Kels. You haven't been yourself, but I thought you were depressed. I wanted to cheer you up. Shit, I bought you a martini. You didn't drink that did you?"

Kelsie snickered. "I'm pretty sure those two guys were wearing what little I'd managed to drink. I'm just glad I didn't try the olive trick that you pulled."

They looked at each other, and burst out giggling like a pair of sixteen year olds.

"The baby is Marq's. Right?"

Kelsie nodded as they walked up the steps back to their front door. "I..we..I think one of the condoms broke."

She ignored the side-eye that Alice shot her.

Inside their apartment, she poured herself a small glass of ginger ale. It helped a little with her stomach. Mostly it helped clear the awful taste from her mouth.

"Was he served the divorce papers already?"

Kelsie concentrated on watching the bubbles in her glass float to the top and pop for a few seconds before answering. The words felt like a confession. "They are all ready to send. I keep meaning to. I just haven't."

"And he doesn't know about the baby?"

She closed her eyes, avoiding the look on her friend's face. "No. You are the first person I've told. I wasn't even admitting it to myself."

"He has rights...."

Kelsie sighed. "Yes, I know all about his rights. I've had that class too, remember? I will tell him. I promise I will tell him. Unless..."

"Unless what?" asked Alice softly.

Unless he didn't want the baby. Unless it would just further mess up his life. Unless she gave it up for adoption or... She couldn't bring herself to contemplate that "or". "Unless nothing. I should make a doctor's appointment."

"Yeah, you should. What are you going to do about school?"

Kelsie smiled. "I'm done with all my classes but one in December. I think the baby is due in May or June. I can still graduate and take the bar and everything."

"And find a job?"

"Can I just focus on one day at a time for now?" The words came out faster, harsher than she expected.

Alice recoiled, and Kelsie immediately regretted snapping. Instead, tears welled up behind her eyes.

"I'm sorry. I don't know what's wrong with me, lately."

Alice hugged her. "Everything is going to be okay. But promise me you will tell Marq about the baby before he signs those papers. I'm advising you as your lawyer. If the judge finds out that you withheld it from him, then you could lose custody. Or worse."

"Tomorrow. I need to go to Mom's and pick up a few things. I will go tell him tomorrow."

CHAPTER ELEVEN

"Can you please do me this favor?"

Marq sighed. Julie crossed her arms over her chest and cocked one hip. She was mad, and he was about to pay for it.

"I can't watch Jo right now. I have work to do." His laptop beeped as another email came in, this one from one of his suppliers, marked urgent. "You know I love him and I'm always happy to help. But I'm way behind on paperwork. Do you want to get paid today or not?"

She sighed dramatically and rolled her eyes. "Can't he just stay in your office and play games on his phone? According to the family court judge, I can't leave him unsupervised. Ever. How am I supposed to get paid if I can't go to work?"

He closed his eyes and rubbed his temples. This argument always went round in circles. Julie was a competent bartender, and he was happy to have her working for him. But the job meant she worked mostly nights. He had tried getting her to take more daytime shifts, or rotate as a server occasionally, but the tips weren't as good. If he even hinted that she should finish her GED and think about a career path with regular office hours, she would either get angry or cry that he was trying to force her out of a job.

The big fight that landed Jo in the hospital happened while he was left home alone. Or rather was supposed to be home alone. Instead he had been out in the school parking lot getting into exactly the sort of trouble that Marq used to at that age. The kind of trouble that started with bravado and a big mouth and ended with Jo taking a swing at an older kid. He was the one knocked unconscious, but since he started the fight, the judge only agreed to keep him out of juvie on the condition that his family situation improve.

"Jo will be really quiet, I promise."

Yeah right. "Fine, he can come in. But I have to get this paperwork done today."

He still had a couple of hours until opening, and the Saturday lunch crowd was not as high-spirited as the dinner and cocktail clientele. With more baby showers and fewer bachelorette parties, Marq usually had some down time to review the books and inventory and make the employee schedule for the next week. He hated doing paperwork on the computer. Some of it was no big deal--planning inventory, ordering supplies, dreaming up specials that would botch entice diners and use up extra ingredients before they spoiled. That was fun. Accounting sucked bad.

He had an accounting firm check over everything once a month. Usually he grumbled that they cost too much and didn't do anything. Until last month.

Right after he and Kelsie got home from Las Vegas, he got his monthly report from the service. There were discrepancies between the numbers from two of the suppliers, his inventory was off, and his overall profit seemed down. They sent back a list of "helpful questions" to help figure out what went wrong. Was there more waste than normal? Change of ingredients? Any large events that weren't recorded correctly?

He had rushed through everything early so he could get on that airplane, so he chalked the problem up to his own sloppiness. But yesterday he got the most recent report. The numbers didn't add up again.

Either he was losing his mind, or someone in the restaurant was stealing from him.

His office door banged open, and Joaquín slouched in then flopped on the ratty old couch he kept along the far wall. "Hey Tío."

Marq schooled his face into a welcoming grin. "Yo, Jo."

"You can quit doing that, you know."

"Doing what?"

Joaquín pulled out a phone and leaned forward, propping his elbows on his knees as his thumbs went to work on the screen. All of a sudden over the summer, he had started stretching out in height and was all limb these days. The boy's face was changing too: his jaw was starting to elongate and take on edges that didn't used to be there. He wasn't as much of a little boy anymore.

"Quit calling me that nickname. It was funny when I was little. Not funny anymore."

Marq pondered that for a minute. He really was growing up. Too fast, way too fast. "How is school? Seventh grade this year?"

"Fine."

"Do you have a favorite class?"

Joaquín grinned at something only he could see on the screen.

"How is your mom holding up?"

Jo quirked an eyebrow at that. "Don't you see her all the time?"

Marq shrugged. "When she's working. And I'm working. Things get pretty crazy around here in the evenings. There hasn't been much time for just talking."

Jo looked back down at his screen. "She's all right I guess. Did she tell you she went to get her hair done?"

"When was that?"

Jo smirked. "Just now. She said her shift

didn't start for another two hours, but you said I could stay here in your office while she was gone."

She left that part out. Marq stood up. "Phone down. We have work to do."

"Huh?"

"Let's go. Its time you learned how a restaurant is run."

For the next hour and a half, he took Joaquín with him as he walked the entire place, back to front. In the walk-in cooler, he made his nephew count jugs of cream, pounds of butter, trays of vegetables, and other supplies while he typed the quantities into a spreadsheet. He showed the kid how to check the freshness dates and to arrange all the shelves so that the oldest supplies were in front and would get used up first.

"What happens if the food goes bad?"

Marq shrugged. "We throw it out. Can't serve rotten eggs. If we are getting really close to the expiration date on some things, we come up with a menu special to feature it. Too much cream, maybe we do crème brulée. If the strawberries are on the brink, we make a sauce out of them to drizzle over the desserts. If there is too much of the prepared food left, sometimes I let the staff take some home, or we donate leftovers to a shelter."

In the freezer, Joaquín whistled appreciatively at the industrial tubs of house-made ice cream. "Can I have a sundae?"

Marq laughed. "After we finish this job, we'll see."

He let Joaquín fill one of the rolling mop buckets with hot water and supervised as he tried to scrub down the floor by the back door. He kept forgetting to squeeze enough extra water out of the mop head, so Marq had to follow up with a dry one to take care of the puddles.

They broke down cardboard boxes and carried them out to the recycling bin. Jo volunteered to make chocolate dipped strawberries, but Sofia, the assistant pastry chef, was too much of a perfectionist to share the job. "We can make those at home later."

Marq found an extra staff T-shirt and had Joaquín pull it on over his shirt and follow him out to the front patio to help set out chairs and open umbrellas before the midday sun turned the cast aluminum furniture into branding irons for the customer's legs.

Finally, they both collapsed at one of the tables and Marq sent one of the hostesses inside for a chocolate sundae. It arrived with a pile of whipped cream on the top nearly as large as the ice cream, and Joaquín dug in like a starving man.

Marq could remember being that age. That was the beginning of being always hungry. His *abuela* would feed him huge bowls of rice and beans. He loved hanging out with her in her kitchen, watching her bustle from one pot to the next. She would talk while she was cooking-- sometimes describing the food, sometimes just jabbering about people or the news or nothing at all. If he volunteered to clean the beaters from the mixer, he got to lick them first. That was a heavenly deal for growing kid.

A shadow passed over the table. "How are my two favorite men?"

Julie bent down to kiss the top of Joaquín's head. Jo brushed off the kiss.

"I hope you didn't fill him up with too many sweets, Marquez Castillo." She shook a finger at him, but her eyes were playful.

Marq smiled. It was good to see her looking less wound up for once. "No worries. I made him work for his treat."

"Tío Marq is teaching me how to run a restaurant." Joaquín scooped another enormous bite of ice cream into his mouth.

Julie put one hand on Marq's shoulder and gave it a light squeeze. She leaned in, bringing with her a haze of hairspray and chemicals, and kissed him on the cheek. "He is so lucky to have you in his life."

There was a question in her eyes, and her shoulder pat turned into a caress. Marq put his hand on hers, squeezed it lightly and then removed it from his shoulder and let it go gently, trying to hide his annoyance.

Julie was a beautiful woman, and she

could be very charming when she wanted to be. But after this morning's emotional manipulation, he didn't want any of her charm turned his way. "We made it work. Joaquín, why don't you finish that up at the bar while your mother gets ready to open. I still have reports to look over."

He straightened up the chairs one more time, dreading what he might find on the computer. Another shadow crossed over him.

"Hi Marq."

Kelsie.

She looked beautiful, as always, with a pair of tight-fitting white capris that showed off the lean muscle of her legs, and an off-the-shoulder tunic that drew his gaze up to her slender neck, to her earlobes that he loved to nibble, to her eyes. Her eyes were uncertain, withdrawn. She clutched a floral backpack to her chest like a shield.

"God, it's good to see you," he said.

She inhaled as though she were working up to a big speech. She had a chunky beaded necklace on. The colors distracted him, drawing his eye down the bare flesh of her upper chest toward where her breasts were hidden behind that backpack.

"Do you want to go inside? We have a fresh pan of brownies."

She glanced towards the door and bit her bottom lip. "I better not. That was Julie with your nephew, right? I don't want to make anyone upset."

Marq's throat tightened. "Yeah. Look, I know I haven't called you the past few weeks..."

She blinked then set her bag down on a table in front of her. She unzipped it and started rifling through it. "I've been busy, too. School. All of the craziness of a new semester. I'm sorry that I am late getting this to you."

She pulled out an envelope and handed it to him, her eyes bright.

The paper was thick and heavy.

"I screwed up," she said, clutching that backpack to herself again. "With the legal paperwork. Before. When I went to get the divorce papers ready, I realized that we actually have to file for a legal separation first."

Divorce. Of course that's why she was here. He clenched his jaw, feeling like he'd been sucker punched. The paper felt like lead in his hand.

"Anyway, if you sign that and get it filed--all the instructions are in there--then you should be all set for taxes at the end of the year. As soon as the time limitation is up, I will send over the actual divorce papers. Around June next year. Okay?"

June. Another six months away. He cleared his throat. "Um, yeah. Sure. Whatever."

"Here," she held out her hand. On her palm lay the white gold and aquamarine ring he had given her.

"No. Keep it."

Her voice wavered. "I can't."

He closed his hand around her fingers, folding them over the ring. Her hands were like ice, and still so soft in his. "What would I need it back for?"

She slowly took her hand back from his. "Okay. Thank you. I..I need to go. I have to stop by Mom's. And I have a big exam coming up this week. And a long drive back."

He nodded. "Yeah. Me too. Lots of work to do."

He didn't watch as she walked away.

Back inside the building, the cool of the air conditioning hit him like a hard freeze. He glanced back through the windows as she climbed behind the steering wheel of her little car. He thought he saw her wipe her eyes.

"Marq, can you come over here?" Julie's voice cut through the fog that had settled over him. "I need you."

Kelsie's fingers still tingled from the touch of Marq's hand, and the tears that had poured down her cheeks as she drove to her mother's house still stung her eyes and cheeks. She pulled into the driveway and let herself in through the garage door.

She heard her mother's startled cry before

she realized what she had just walked into. She stopped cold.

There, in the kitchen, stood her mother and a man. Willard. He had her mother backed up against the built-in wall oven. Mom was shirtless, and her floral skirt was hiked up and above her waist. She still had on the sneakers she wore out on long walks, and a pair of champagne-colored silky underwear were tangled around her ankles. Willard's own shirt seemed to be unbuttoned, and his balding head was pressed to her mother's bare breasts.

"Mom!"

"Kelsie." The word was full of outrage. "What are you doing here?"

Kelsie took a step backwards, turning away from the vision of her mother making out in the kitchen with a man. It was a vision she could never unsee.

"Oh my god. I just came to pick up some clothes from my closet. What are you doing? In the kitchen?? With him???" The roman shade over the kitchen window was up, and she quickly yanked it closed. "The next door neighbors can see right in."

Her mother made a sound of exasperation, and Kelsie could hear the rustling sounds of fabric being straightened. Then the soft wisp of a zipper.

"Excuse me, ladies. I will leave you to your discussion." The words were way too polite and well-mannered to make Kelsie feel any better.

"Thank you, dear," said her mother to him.

Kelsie listened to the man's slow footprints fade toward the living room on the other side of the house.

"Well, what do you have to say for yourself?"

Kelsie bristled. "What do I have to say for myself? Does Helmut know about this?"

Her mother snorted. Actually snorted. "It is none of his business how I spend my time any more than it is yours. This is my house. You need to call before you just barge in."

Kelsie let out a breath that bordered on quavery. "I just wanted to come pick up some clothes."

Her mother gave her a level look. "Absolutely. You have your own apartment to keep things in. In fact, take all your clothes. And the rest of your belongings. Stop treating my house like a storage unit."

"Fine." Kelsie crossed her arms over her chest, not bothering to make sure the loose folds of her top didn't show the slight round bulge of her belly. Not that her mother noticed.

"Fine." Her mother turned and walked out of the kitchen.

Fighting alternating waves of nausea, indignation, and shame, Kelsie made several trips to and from her car with armfuls of clothes and shoes and books from her childhood room. She didn't pack anything, didn't sort. Just grabbed and dumped them into her trunk, then into the backseat once the trunk was full.

She didn't stop until her closet was empty and her shoulders ached from all of the carrying. Sweat trickled down her temples and spine, and her toes were sore where her decorative little flip flops rubbed against the skin. Mom and Willard had disappeared out the front door earlier without a word.

Hefting a cardboard box filled with her princess figurines, she gave her old room one last look. Dust bunnies swirled in the air over a desk that had been cleared. The shelves were empty. The bed neatly made. It looked like a girly guest room, which, she supposed, it now was.

The princesses were the only things she had packed neatly, wrapping each one into a T-shirt so they didn't break on her way home. *Home*. The thought of her shared apartment becoming her actual home made her nausea rise again. She gave one last glance around the old room. Time to go home.

CHAPTER TWELVE

Marq was almost certain he knew who was stealing from him, and the knowledge was killing him.

He stood back just inside the entrance to the kitchen where he had a clear view of the front door and about half of the dining room. He and a couple of the staff members had spent Black Friday hanging white and gold Christmas lights from the exposed rafters. Merry diners with shopping bags propped by their feet sipped from mugs of cinnamon cocoa and plates of *cajeta*-topped chocolate shortbread cookies on the tables in front of them. Despite the eighty-five degree South Florida weather, the restaurant was doing a brisk business in hot drinks.

Sofia puttered around behind him, adding tiny star and bell decorations to one of half a dozen tall cakes lined up on the counter. She talked to the cakes as she worked, calling them pet names and occasionally swearing in a slurry of words that made him blush and laugh at the same time. The woman was brilliant with icing and fondant and modeling chocolate, could easily handle most of the kitchen management when he wasn't around, and was completely self-taught. And she was likely a thief.

The knowledge ground at him like sand in the swim trunks. He liked Sofia. He needed Sofia. And she needed this job.

She had two teenagers still at home, he knew, plus an elderly grandmother. He was pretty sure she was their primary means of support. She had three older children as well, all adults. At least one was still in Mexico. When he'd first hired her, there was a boyfriend in the picture, one who glowered and hovered and honked his horn angrily outside if she didn't rush to his car the second her shift was done. But the boyfriend disappeared--jailed, or so the staff gossip claimed--and so did the occasional purple bruise she used to sport on her upper arms or near her temples.

He originally hired her as a bartender, but she and Julie did not get along at all, which surprised him. Sofia was older than Julie by nearly twenty years, and didn't take well to the younger woman giving her instructions. And when Julie felt like her place in the restaurant was threatened, she went on the offensive. Instead of allowing Julie to run Sofia off, he'd given her work in the kitchen in the mornings, helping him with the day's baking. It wasn't long before she had taken over most of it herself.

"Con permiso."

Sofia's voice startled him out of his reverie. He stepped aside as she hefted a sheet pan with two of her finished confections past him, headed for the glass display case out front. Marq gave her a brief smile as she passed, then turned on a heel and sulked into his office.

With the door closed safely behind him, he slumped into his chair. His laptop screen taunted him, so he flipped it shut. Finally he pulled out his phone and dialed.

Wei picked up after a handful of rings. "Yeah?"

"I need some advice." Marq could hear the familiar cacophony of a commercial kitchen in the background. He cringed, realizing that he'd caught Wei working. "I'm having trouble with an employee."

Wei listened to the short version of the story. "I can find you another pastry chef, no problem."

Marq hesitated. "What if I don't want to fire her?"

There was a sound in the background of the phone like china breaking. "Why not? She's hurting your bottom line. I might know some folks looking for work. Let me send you a couple of names, okay? And call your lawyer. Make sure that you don't get yourself sued when you can her ass."

Typical Wei, measuring success in dollars and culinary reviews. Yes, Marq wanted both. But to achieve that at the cost of someone like Sofia and her family. It just didn't sit well, missing supplies or not. "Um, okay. That would be great. I guess. Thanks."

He clicked off the phone and stared at his bulletin board for a long time. He had covered it with photos that meant a lot to him--shots of the restaurant's renovation, of Joaquín, of himself and his *abeula* in her kitchen when he was just a kid. There had to be something else he could try. Surely there was another way he could solve this.

He dialed again, and held his breath as it rang.

As soon as he heard Kelsie's voice on the other end of the line, he exhaled.

"I need some advice," he said

A pause. "From me?"

"Yeah. Legal advice, kind of."

"I haven't graduated or taken the bar exam yet. I can't give you legal advice." Her voice sounded a little strange. Quieter than normal, less happy than she was over the summer.

He picked up a pen, twirled it, then stopped and set it down carefully. "I know. I don't need a regular lawyer. Just advice. It's about one of my employees."

"Um, okay. I will try. What's going on?"

He let the story spill out. How the inventory numbers looked off. How he started dou-ble-checking the shelves himself. How things would go missing--a few gallons of milk here, a few vegetables there. How his accountant had pointed out that rising costs were eating into his profits.

"Wait," she interrupted. "You have an ac-countant, but not a lawyer?"

He pushed to his feet, keeping the phone to his ear. Paced the short length of his office. "Yeah, well, I spent too much time in court-rooms with lawyers. Most of them are assholes."

"Gee, thanks." Her voice was flat.

He felt a catch in his chest as he realized what he had said and tried to take it back. "Not you. Never you. Prosecuting attorneys are the assholes. You're not like them at all. Just, okay, this isn't going well is it?"

She sighed audibly. When she spoke, her voice was softer. "I get why you would have trouble trusting some people. Don't worry about that part. So, what kind of advice do you need about the theft? Do you know who is doing it? Have you reported it to the police?"

He rested his head against the wall in front of where he stood. "I know who is doing it. The missing items only seem to disappear when one particular employee is on duty. Usually when she is in early to work before everyone else."

There was a faint noise like wind, or an

intake of breath through the connection. "Who is she? Did you fire her? Did you call the police on her?"

"I can't. I don't want to. This is where I need that almost-lawyer advice."

"Marq, I told you--"

"I know you're not a lawyer yet. But I thought you might be able to sympathize. The problem is that the lady in question is a single mother."

Another pause. Another response barely louder than a whisper. "Oh. A mother."

Marq's throat tightened as he considered how much else to reveal. "And it's not just her kids that I'm worried about."

"Kids? More than one?" Her voice sounded almost like a squeak.

"Yeah. Teenagers, I think. I know how hard it is for kids that age alone on the street. But it's worse than that."

"Okay, that sucks. But the suspense is killing me here. She's a single mother stealing food for a couple of hungry teenagers. How does it get worse?" she asked.

"I think she's an illegal immigrant."

Kelsie's stomach flipped at Marq's words and she sat down hard on the couch, her hand on her expanding belly. She was going to be sick.

Or she was going to burst out in tears. Maybe both at once. Goodness knew she had endured plenty of episodes of both lately.

The anguish in Marq's voice was all too obvious even over the phone, and she couldn't blame him. The more he shared about his suspected-thief, the more her heart ached for the woman and for Marq. From his description of her, the woman sounded like an angel. Possibly abused but strong and independent and funny. She found herself chuckling along with him as he told her about some of the nicknames she'd given other members of the staff. What a horrible quandary.

The brief moment of laugher cleared some of the crazy pregnancy emotions from clouding her brain as she mentally reviewed what she'd learned in an employment law last year. It wasn't just the woman's (and her kids') future she was worried about.

She took a deep breath and steeled herself for what she knew she had to do.

"So you think she might really be in trouble?" he asked.

"It's not just that. Listen, Marq, I think you could be in deep trouble here."

"Me?"

"First of all, don't tell this story to anyone else, unless it is to a real lawyer. If you hired someone even after you knew, or even suspected, that she was here illegally, you can be held liable too. You could lose your business license or worse. If you start talking to people about hiring illegal immigrants, then someone could turn you in. Testify against you"

He was quiet on the other end. "And would you? Testify against me?"

She grimaced as she felt another flip in her belly. She had been getting those more and more often lately. At first it felt like gas, which she had more of than she wanted to admit. But sometimes that little bubble wasn't gas. It was a kick, she was almost sure. She moved her hand a little lower, and felt it again.

"No, I wouldn't have to." The tears she'd been holding back sneaked around her defenses after all. "No judge would make me testify. I can't be your lawyer, but legally I am still your wife."

CHAPTER THIRTEEN

Kelsie adjusted the straps of her back-pack, wincing as they dug into the sides of her already sore breasts. Her ob-gyn had suggested that she get a bag with wheels soon and stop carrying loads on her back. It was great advice, except that she still had to heft her books up and down the steps to her apartment every day. Elevators weren't exactly on her and Alice's priority lists when they had first moved in three years ago. Besides, she only had two final exams left to go before Christmas break next week, and next semester she only had a one real class left to graduate. Surely she wouldn't get so fat that she couldn't carry around one single textbook.

"You have a gentleman caller."

"Good afternoon, Mrs. Martin." Kelsie forced a smile. "How are you feeling today?"

Deborah Martin, Kelsie's downstairs neighbor, stood in the crack of her own apartment door. Her gray hair was styled, as usual, in one of those curly helmet looks that required a trip to the beauty salon and an entire can of hair spray. She wore a yellow house coat and fleece slippers beneath a disapproving frown. "I am fine, thank you. That young man of yours knocked on my door over an hour ago. Had the wrong apartment number. He has been waiting for you ever since."

Kelsie's stomach tightened almost painfully. On the phone the day before yesterday, Marq had tried to convince her to drive up and have dinner with him. She didn't quite lie about having too much studying for final exams to do. He offered to come here, and she tried to explain how busy her schedule was, between class and a group project, and her tutoring job. She thought he had given up when he finally asked if he could call again in a couple of days to tell her what he found out about the theft.

The thought of him standing upstairs filled her with dread.

"In my day, young ladies did not accept gentlemen callers without a chaperone."

Kelsie almost rolled her eyes. The woman wasn't that old. By her calculations, Deborah Martin could easily have enjoyed most of the free love days of the sixties before meeting the late Mr. Martin. "Luckily for me times have changed for the better."

Deborah cast a knowing look at Kelsie's rounding belly, thrust even farther forward than normal by the weight of books on her back.

"Don't keep your young man waiting."

Maybe it's better to get this over with now. Kelsie took a deep breath and started up the stairs, one hand on the railing. Her balance was getting off lately too. The last thing she needed was to literally fall at Marq's feet.

She was only slightly out of breath by the time she reached the top step and saw his shadow. He had his back to the sun at first, so she couldn't quite see his features. Then he turned.

A hot blush crept up her face that had nothing to do with her efforts on the stairs and everything to do with her belly. She took another step forward and saw sandy brown hair that badly needed a cut curling around his ears. Familiar green eyes.

He wore well-worn dark khaki pants and a white button down shirt--the outdoorsy kind that hikers wore to keep the sun off, not the stiffly pressed business suit version. On the ground next to him was a florist box.

"Kelsie."

It wasn't Marq. *It wasn't Marq.*

"Rob. What are you doing here?" She dropped her bag unceremoniously and rushed forward to her brother's outstretched arms.

He held her tight for a minute, resting his chin on top of her shoulder. She remembered when her head used to tuck under his chin.

After a moment, he pulled back and looked down at the front of her. "I guess I'm not the only one with a surprise today."

She unlocked the door while he gathered her backpack and a dusty suitcase and followed her in. He held out the flowers. "Where do you want these?"

"Um, maybe on the kitchen table? That was really nice of you. Help yourself to a drink. Water glasses above the sink, or there might be a soda or something in the fridge."

He shrugged. "Don't thank me, they were waiting on your doorstep when I got here. Your neighbor lady is pretty nosy."

She checked the shipping label on the front of the flower box. They were addressed to her, not Alice. "Yeah. She doesn't get out much. I don't know if she is more fascinated or scandalized by having two single women law students living upstairs."

"You and Alice are both single then?"

Kelsie ripped into the box, ignoring the obvious innuendo in his question. There was no good way to answer that question directly without a lie or the insane truth. Out of the delivery package, she extracted a beautiful emerald green pot filled with white roses alternating with deep red poinsettias. Below the plants was another gift box with a small card taped to it. The box was covered in foil wrapping with the Chocolate, Chocolate logo printed on it.

She tore open the wrapper. Inside was a tray of thick fudgy brownies with the icing on top. The same kind Marq fed her that day when she first stumbled into him.

"So," Rob said, popping the top on a can of Coke. "I take it those are from him?"

Kelsie flushed and half turned away so she could read the card without him seeing it over her shoulder. "Him who?"

Rob snorted. "I'm neither blind nor stupid."

Love, Marq. Two tiny words, in his handwriting, stole her breath.

She stuffed the card into her pocket and sat down on the couch. Her brother set his can down on a coaster and collapsed onto the other end. He ran his fingers through that too-long hair and sighed. He looked tanner, leaner, and older. The lines on his face were sharper, the curve of his jaw less rounded. He had just the start of fine lines around his eyes.

"When did you get home?" she asked.

"I just landed this morning. Who's the daddy?"

She shook her head. "I'd rather not talk about him."

He raised one eyebrow. "Let me guess, you got in a fight and stormed off? And he's sending flowers trying to make it up to you?"

That might have been true of the old her, but not this one. Not the one who walked willingly away from a guy like Marq. She closed her eyes for a second, and hoped Rob would think she were agreeing with his guess. "Does Mom know you're here?"

"Does Mom know you're pregnant?"

"No."

"Does Helmut?"

She laughed bitterly. "Both Helmut and Mom told me to grow up and learn to take care of myself. So I am."

He considered her for a second, then took another long drink of his Coke. "Me, too."

"We are such a dysfunctional family," she said.

"I'll drink to that." He held up his can in a mock toast.

Kelsie burst into tears.

He wrapped an arm around her and pulled her over to cry on his shoulder. It took her way longer to get herself together than she expected. Every time she tried to take a deep breath and will herself to stop crying, another wave of emotion would hit her and she started bawling even harder. Rob just kept patting her hair and whispering that it would be okay.

"I'm sorry," she said when the worst of the sobbing finally subsided. "Stupid hormones."

He half-smiled. "It's okay. That's what shoulders are for."

"Why did you come home? Did something happen? Not that I want you to leave, because I don't. I'm just surprised."

He took a long time answering. "Things in Rio got complicated. And my research may be on hold for the time being. I needed to get out of there for a while."

The door burst open and Alice bustled in. "Are you home, Kelsie? Wait until you hear about the new librarian in the law library. I would swear he's the underwear model from that catalog..."

Alice stopped short at the site of Kelsie and Rob cuddled on the couch.

"Are you..." she never finished the question.

Rob stood up and offered Alice his right hand. "Rob Forrester. I'm Kelsie's brother."

Her eyes flew wide, and Kelsie watched in some amusement as her friend gave Rob *the look*. The same one she had probably given the poor new guy at the library earlier today.

"You're the brother from the jungle!"

Rob shrugged. "I only wear the loincloth for special events."

Alice gave him the look again. Kelsie cleared her throat.

Alice looked from Rob to Kelsie and back again, the mouthed the words "Does he know" with exaggerated lip motions.

Kelsie rolled her eyes, stood up, stretched, and rubbed her belly. The kicking feeling was back, on the opposite side this time from yesterday. "Yes, he knows that I'm pregnant. It isn't that hard to figure out, you know."

Kelsie set down her fork, feeling both disappointed and embarrassed that she had cleaned her plate. Not even a crust from her French bread was left. She'd used the heel to sop up some more of the meaty spaghetti sauce left after her noodles had vanished. Across her tiny kitchen table, Rob had done a similar job on his dinner. Alice had only picked at hers, and completely avoided the garlic bread.

"You have no idea how much I have missed good American home cooking," Rob said, rubbing his belly.

Alice raised one eyebrow. "You know this is sauce from a jar, right?"

Kelsie stuck her tongue out at her friend, and they both dissolved into a fit of giggles. The giggles soon gave way to a loud belch, and she felt her face flame.

Rob laughed even harder.

"Oh, just stop. I can't help it. The books say that all pregnant women have that problem."

"I'm sorry, Kelsie. But when my baby sister can out-belch half of my college fraternity...that is funny."

Alice's cheeks were pink and her eyes glowed with the wine that she had split with

Rob. Kelsie was a little jealous of that, but her brother had given her a sip. Kelsie felt another hiccup threatening and set her hand on the top of her rounding belly trying to talk herself out of it. Good thing she couldn't actually drink much alcohol. Even though morning sickness was supposed to fade after her first trimester, food still sometimes came back up when she least expected it. She had quite enjoyed that small sip of wine and really didn't want to know what it tasted like on the rebound.

"I should probably tell Mom I'm in the country," Rob said after their mirth had faded down to a pleasant round of smiles.

"She doesn't know yet?"

Alice jumped in, "Where are you staying tonight?"

"I hadn't really thought that far ahead."

"Just so you know, the last time I went to Mom's unannounced, I got thrown out of the house. You can crash here if you need to."

Rob frowned. "What do you mean she threw you out?"

Kelsie couldn't suppress a sigh. "I didn't think about calling before I went to the house I wanted to pick up some more of my clothes--looking for something that still fit, you know."

Alice raised an eyebrow. "That was the day you went to go see--"

"My doctor," Kelsie said with a sharp look at her roommate. "Anyway, Mom and her boyfriend were..." She couldn't quite bring herself to finish that sentence.

But a wine-fueled Alice could. "Your mom was messing around in the kitchen and Kelsie walked in on them. They got in a fight, and she cried on my shoulder for two days."

Kelsie slunk down in her chair and ignored Rob's eyes on her.

"So Mom has a boyfriend, huh. Do you have room on your couch? I can call in the morning and make sure the coast is clear before I drive home."

"Ooh!" squealed Alice from the kitchen. "He sent you brownies. Why can't my men ever send me chocolate?"

Kelsie froze.

Rob grinned. "Sounds like your mysterious guy knows the way to your heart. What did this one do that was so terrible? Did he abandon you on the side of the road somewhere?"

"Shut up, Rob."

Alice came around the corner, laughing around the large forkful of chocolate she was stuffing into her mouth.

"Hey now, those were for me."

Alice rolled her eyes and brought the whole pan to the table with a knife. "I just wanted one bite. I see why that restaurant is so famous for its desserts. Maybe you should keep stringing him along. Brownies could be just the start. And no, Rob, this guy hasn't left her on the side of the road. Yet."

Kelsie glared at him. "Drop it, Alice."

"Let's see, I have picked you up at least..." Alice screwed up her slightly flushed face and counted on her fingers, "Four different times when you walked out on a date and needed a ride. And that doesn't count Sam-Steve-what-was-his-name? The one where Helmut rescued you?"

"Scott," Kelsie ground out.

"Oh yeah. Scott. Who left you in the middle of a cornfield."

Kelsie felt her face flush to match Alice's, but hers was not the wine. "I left him. And it was at a rest stop in Peoria, Illinois. Not exactly a cornfield."

Alice grinned. "That's right. Helmut came to save you that day. And then there was Zach this summer. He left you at the beach and stole your shoes."

Kelsie picked up the knife and cut herself a wedge of brownie. Her stomach gave a little rumble, though she wasn't sure if it was hunger or acid reflux. "Zach didn't steal my shoes. I forgot they were in his truck when I told him to get lost."

"And then you had to walk home barefoot." Alice licked icing off one finger.

Kelsie ignored Rob's amused glances and focused on cutting him his own slice of brownie. "Yeah, lucky me I ran into an old friend who called me a cab."

"Lucky you is right. That's the day you met..." Alice must have finally noticed the expression on Kelsie's face and quit talking.

"Met who?" asked Rob, taking a bite of his dessert. "Anyone I know?"

"The baby's father. And I'm done talking about this for now, okay. You can crash on our couch. There are blankets and an extra pillow in the closet. I'm going to bed."

CHAPTER FOURTEEN

"Here, catch." Marq tossed a baseball mitt to Joaquín.

His nephew swatted it out of the air and threw it right back. "No thanks, Tío. Not in the mood."

"Hey, Yo-Jo, what's the matter? Last day of school until after New Year's, the weather's beautiful, and you're sulking like..." Marq caught himself before calling him a "surly teen-ager". That was way too close to the truth.

"I'm not sulking," said Joaquín with his lower jaw jutted out and balled fists buried deep in his jeans pockets.

Marq tucked the mitt into his own and stuffed them under one arm, trying to hide the disappointment he felt. He had been watching the clock all through lunch rush waiting for his nephew to get off school so they could go hang out at the park. "How about a walk?"

"Whatever."

Marq motioned at the paved jogging path

that wound through stands of magnolia trees in bloom. He held his tongue for several long minutes. Joaquín's shoulders drooped underneath an oversized T-shirt, and he dragged his slightly-too-big-feet.

"When do you get your report card? How were your grades?"

Joaquín shrugged and mumbled, "Okay, I guess."

Uh oh. "What about basketball? Your mom said you were trying out for the seventh grade team."

Joaquín kicked at rock and sent it flying across the path and into a small patch of flowers. "I decided not to."

"I'm surprised. I thought you were looking forward to it."

"Basketball is a dumb sport."

The words echoed in Marq's head as they walked. He knew those words. Knew that kick. Knew the way Joaquín kept his emotions hidden deep inside beneath the slumped shoulders and the attitude. Knew that the attitude was just the warm-up act for the full-on aggression he would start feeling soon.

Marq knew the feeling. He had lived it when he was Joaquín's age.

But what he couldn't puzzle out was why. Marq's father had abandoned him. His mother dead. He slept on a revolving series of couches in other people's homes.

Joaquín had his mother. He had an apartment, school clothes, plenty of food. Marq himself had bought him a brand new pair of basketball shoes when Julia had mentioned that Joaquín was trying out for the team. Sure, it wasn't the kind of life you saw on breakfast cereal commercials, with Mom and Dad and little sister in an immaculate suburban kitchen. But it was way better than it could have been.

They walked. With each step, Marq felt more and more powerless to help.

They stopped at a bridge looking over a small creek. Marq leaned his forearms on the railing, and Joaquín picked up rocks and began hurling them into the water one by one. "I wish you would marry my mom and be my dad for real."

Marq forced what he hoped was a light-hearted chuckle. "You haven't said that to me for years."

"Yeah. When I was little, I used to think you *were* my dad."

Marq crooked a half-smile. Joaquín was still little, to him. He ruffled his nephew's hair, and Joaquín didn't even duck out of the way.

"Remember what I always told you when you were *little*. Your real dad was a wonderful man."

He hoped that Joaquín didn't notice how he stumbled over "man". They were just kids when his cousin died. But Joaquín Senior was more man than Marq had been back then.

"I always want you to remember how much he loved you, even though he never got to meet you. I can never replace that. But I am your family, forever and always."

Joaquín frowned. "And if my mom marries someone else? What happens then?"

"Nothing happens. I will still be your Tío Marq. And then you also get a stepfather. You get two of us looking out for you, not just one."

Joaquín's shoulders slouched another notch lower. "That's not what José says."

Marq straightened up and crossed his arms over his chest. "Who is José?"

"Mom's boyfriend. He stays over a lot. I don't like him."

Marq's chest constricted at the anguish in Joaquín's voice. Kids get jealous when their parents date, he told himself. And change makes them nervous. "Oh yeah? Surely he can't be that bad. Does this José make your mother smile?"

Joaquín shook his head. "I guess so. But he also says that things are going to change for me. And when Mom isn't there, he's mean to me."

"Mean, how?"

"He makes me do stuff for him. And he takes away my stuff when he says I'm misbehaving."

Marq almost laughed out loud in relief. "A few chores never hurt anyone. Let's keep walking and leave a few rocks for the next person."

The jogging trail led them to stone steps down to a strip of beach. The not-quite-setting sun was just starting to dip behind the buildings that lined the strip across the street, casting long shadows across the sand. Offshore, yellowing light glinted off the dusky blue-green water.

He and Joaquín pulled off their sneakers and socks, tied the laces together, and slung them over shoulders so they could wriggle their toes in the still-warm sand. Jo rolled his jeans legs up and waded ahead through the water, while Marq stuck closer to the edge of the tide. A large wave crashed up and over the boy's knees, soaking his jeans to the thigh.

Joaquín sputtered and Marq laughed. Joaquín scooped his hands together and threw seawater--and a large chunk of seaweed--right at Marq.

"You asked for it now," Marq said with a grin. He dropped his shoes and the baseball mitts far out of reach of the water and paddled both hands back and forth, dousing Joaquín until they both laughed so hard that Marq's abs ached.

"Race you to the pier, Tío," Joaquín shouted, already half a dozen strides ahead.

Marq took off after him, trying to make up the distance by sticking to the sand instead of the water. It took him longer than he had expected. He still had the advantage of size, but Joaquín was growing fast. By the time he was done growing, he would be as tall as or taller than Marq. In the final few yards of their race, Joaquín splashed past a guy who was sat on the sand, staring off into the distance.

Marq pulled up short as the man stood up. "Hey, I'm sorry about that, man. You okay?"

The man brushed water off his face and gave his slightly-shaggy sun-bleached hair a shake. "No problem. Kids will be kids...Marq? Is that you?"

Marq did a double-take. The other guy's hair was longer, his face more worn. But his eyes were the same as ever. Smiling and green and just like Kelsie's. He felt a double-punch to his gut. "Rob Forrester. How long have you been home?"

"Only a couple of days. How have you been?"

They eyed each other warily. Marq felt the weight of all that had passed between them-- the years of friendship, high school experimenta- tion with drugs, the car accident, all that fol- lowed--like a wall of sandbags holding back the flood waters. Rob didn't even know the half of it. He didn't know about Kelsie.

"Um. Great. I have a restaurant on the strip. *Chocolate, Chocolate*. You should stop by sometime."

Rob ran a hand through his hair, a half-smile on his face. "You? A restaurant? That's awesome. You always did have a thing for sweets."

Marq smiled. "Still do."

"Remember the time my baby sister talked you into making her cookies? I found you sitting with her in the back yard and she had chocolate smeared from ear to ear. She followed us around all that summer after that, and pouted every time I told her to get lost."

Marq's mouth went dry. "I remember. You know, I ran into her a while back."

Rob quirked one eyebrow. "Kelsie? How long ago was that?"

Marq shrugged, trying to act casual. "At the end of the summer. She's not a little girl anymore."

"No, she is not." Rob said slowly.

Marq felt the weight of Rob's scrutiny. Kelsie had said that her brother never got their messages about Vegas. But how much had he heard since then? The fact that Rob's fists were nowhere near Marq's face made him think that maybe, just maybe, Rob didn't know much.

Just then, Joaquín came running back toward them. Rob nodded his head. "Is he yours?"

Marq shook his head. "He's my--"

"Tío, where'd you go?" Joaquín stopped next to the two men. He was dripping from head to toe, with a goofy grin on his face.

"Rob, I'd like you to meet my nephew.

Not technically my nephew, but close enough. This is Joaquín. Jo, Rob is an old friend of mine."

Rob froze and stared at the boy for a long moment. Marq saw the color drain from his old friend's face as recognition dawned. He offered his hand. "Joaquín. Nice to meet you."

Joaquín glanced between Marq and Rob, clearly aware of the tension, but not understanding. He gave Rob's hand a cursory shake. "I need to go dry off."

"Okay. Can you go get our shoes? I'll be there in a minute."

Marq and Rob watched as Joaquín splashed back towards the park.

"Is he really..." Rob's voice trailed off.

"Yeah. You remember Julia, right? She works for me now. Joaquín's a good kid."

After another long pause, Rob finally broke the silence. "I was gone way too long."

"Does that mean you're back to stay?" Marq didn't know whether he really wanted the answer to that question.

"I'm not sure yet. It looks like the boy likes you."

Joaquín was waving furiously at him. Marq smiled, reassured by the antics. "Yes, he does. Hey, it's good to see you. Stop by the restaurant sometime and we can talk. About old times."

Marq offered his hand to Rob. He didn't miss the pause and the frown right before Rob clasped it in his own. Marq was still wearing his work T-shirt, his forearms bare. There was no way Rob could have missed the tattoos that circled his forearms. Marq clenched his teeth, wondering if Rob knew what they meant.

"I will try. It looks like we have both had an interesting few years."

CHAPTER FIFTEEN

Kelsie knew she would have to face her family sooner or later. She and Mom still were not speaking, though, and if it weren't Christmas Eve, she would happily sit home and watch Alice drink wine.

Rob insisted that she come. And Alice insisted that she leave the apartment and not sit and brood. So here she was.

She glanced at the lights in the living room of her mother's house, her childhood home. The Christmas tree had been set up in the front window as usual, and on the porch stood the four-foot tall light-up plastic Santa Claus that had been there every year since she was little. Saint Nick had a dent in one leg where Rob had hit it with a baseball when he was thirteen, allegedly accidentally.

Taking a deep breath, she set her hand on a spot on her belly where she felt that fluttery tap-tap-tap of the baby. The kicks were getting stronger now, more regular. More real.

She knew how this would go. She would be treated to gasps of horror. Then a million condescending questions. "Don't you know how these things happen?" "How could you be so irresponsible?" Or, her personal favorite: "When will you learn?"

There was an unfamiliar car parked in the driveway. Maybe Rob had rented one. Or it could be Willard. She swallowed down a sudden rise of heartburn at the thought. The last time she saw the man, he had his pants around his ankles.

"Well, kid," she said to her belly. "I guess it's time we make an appearance."

She forced a deep inhale, then an exhale, and got out of the car.

She made it to the front door without dropping the bottle of wine or her purse or the pretty fresh greenery wreath she bought from a street vendor this morning or the giant tub of gingerbread cookies she had baked yesterday. The cookies were one of the few real from-scratch recipes she ever learned to make well. Alice had scolded her for tasting the raw cookie dough. She shouldn't have bothered, because it obviously didn't agree with the baby either. The last tray in the oven burned because she was stuck heaving over the toilet in the bathroom.

The front door opened before she could quite get a hand free, and she nearly tumbled inside into Rob's arms. He smelled like soap and saltwater and coffee and nothing like the sickly-sweet-smoke that used to cling to him in high school. He smelled like the big brother she had spent the last decade missing.

"Let me take that for you. What did you do, pack your entire apartment?"

Kelsie smiled and let her brother take the packages from her.

"Everyone's in the kitchen."

She stopped in the archway from the living room and gulped. When Rob said "everyone", he meant *everyone*.

Her mother was seated at the kitchen table. Willard appeared to be rummaging through one of the cabinets. Helmut stood nearby, wearing his customary sharply creased dress slacks, tailored crisp white shirt, and a scowl. His fiancée, Claire, leaned on the breakfast counter, her shoes already kicked off in some forgotten corner, nursing a glass of wine.

A lump formed in her throat. If only Helmut would hug her like Rob had just done. But the tension in the kitchen was thick and cold.

Claire's eyes lit with a smile. "Kelsie, you made it."

Kelsie let her sister-in-law-to-be give her a hug, and hugged back. Claire glanced down at Kelsie's midsection and back up, eyebrows raised. Kelsie felt her cheeks flush.

"You had a busy semester," Claire said with an almost whisper.

Kelsie huffed. "I guess you could say that."

"Did someone forget to tell me?" asked Claire, taking Kelsie's hands in her own. Claire's fingers were warm on Kelsie's icy ones.

Even with her sensibly flat shoes, Kelsie still towered over Claire's shorter frame. But Claire was the CEO of a successful aerospace company, and despite her habit of going barefoot whenever possible, she still intimidated Kelsie.

Back in undergrad, before Claire and Helmut met, Kelsie had written a short biography on Claire's career as a cutting edge female entrepreneur-turned-executive. Kelsie was a little starstruck the first time her brother introduced them. And later amused when she learned that Claire had been jealous of *her*. Claire had once assumed that Kelsie was Helmut's date, not his sister.

Kelsie shook her head. "The only one who knows is Rob, and only because he flew into Miami first and dropped by my apartment."

Claire gave her hand a squeeze. "Okay. Well, I hate to tell you this, but this hasn't exactly been the friendliest of gatherings. Your news ought to make things...interesting."

"Thanks for the warning. Maybe I should just get this over with. Can I borrow your wine glass and that spoon?"

"Allow me." Claire tapped the spoon on

the glass, filling the room with the ringing.

Despite feeling hot and flushed, Kelsie rubbed her bare arms for warmth as every eye in the room swiveled towards where she stood.

She gulped. Then tried to picture herself defending an innocent client in front of a hostile jury. She straightened her spine and set a hand on top of her baby bump. "Merry Christmas. Surprise, I'm pregnant."

No one spoke. Willard's mouth dropped open. Her mother's pursed into a tight line. Helmut's scowl deepened and focused straight on her. She could feel their shock and disapproval and her own self-pity dragging her downward until she felt dizzy.

"Rob, could you please bring me a glass of water? I need to go sit down."

With her heart pounding and her mind blank with fear, she retreated to the living room and sat in her father's old ugly recliner. She shoved down the side lever, and, with a squeak, the footrest raised up. She contemplated her feet, which had recently started swelling if she stood for too long. Her toenails needed a fresh coat of polish, but it was getting more and more awkward to reach them. Paying for a pedicure seemed too indulgent after the sticker shock of maternity clothes shopping. She sucked in her breath a little and braced for the storm to come.

One by one, the rest of the family followed her into the living room and arrayed themselves on various pieces of furniture. Rob brought her that glass of water and then leaned up against the opposite wall rather than sitting.

Her mother broke the silence "So, do you still expect to graduate?"

Kelsie exhaled a short breath. "The baby is due late May. Hopefully right after graduation, not before."

Claire interrupted. "How are you feeling? Has the baby started to kick? Is it a boy or a girl? Do you need anything to eat?"

Helmut turned to his fiancée and scowled. How many different scowls did her brother have, anyway?

"I am fine right now, thank you. I have been sick off and on, but nothing the doctor is worried about. Yes, the baby is starting to kick." Kelsie started counting silently, willing her eyes to stay dry. She made it to fifteen before anyone else said a word.

Willard slapped one hand on his thigh. "Well, congratulations young lady. Please forgive all of us for being so rude. We were having a, well, a disagreement of sorts before you arrived. We weren't expecting such lovely news, right Edna?"

"How do you expect to take care of a baby when you have never had a full-time job? When you can barely keep track of your car keys?" asked Helmut.

"Leave her alone," growled Rob.

"Don't tell me what to do," snapped Helmut. "I am tired of cleaning up the messes that the two of you leave behind."

"Helmut," Claire warned, placing a hand on his shoulder. He shrugged it off.

"I never asked you to clean up anything of mine," said Rob quietly. "In fact, I asked you to get the hell out of my life. Don't blame us for your choices."

Helmut stood up and took a step toward Rob. "You have no idea what I have done for you."

"Stop it, both of you." Kelsie couldn't help the tears that pooled in her eyes. Damn pregnancy hormones. Damn Alice for talking her into coming. And damn her family for hating each other. She shoved the footrest closed and stood up so fast that her vision got starry and she had to sit back down again, hard. She tried to swallow, but it came out as a giant sob.

Claire tugged on Helmut's hand and he sat. Rob just stayed where he was on the wall and didn't move.

Kelsie stood up again, more slowly this time, and the stars stayed blissfully away. "I knew this was a mistake. I'm going home."

"You can't leave now. It's late, and it's a long drive back to school. You don't need to drive yourself after dark," said her mother.

Kelsie ignored her and started for the door.

"So now I bet you expect us to take you in and provide for the baby. Who is the father, anyway? Let me guess, he is another one of your useless playboys who left you the moment things got rough," growled Helmut.

"Give her a break. Kelsie, don't go. Helmut is only mad because he loves you," said Claire.

Kelsie didn't see the elbow to his ribs, but heard him grunt in pain. She almost smiled, but she kept walking.

Rob caught her at the doorway and handed Kelsie her purse. "I can drive you. I could use the fresh air."

"Stop, both of you. Please."

Kelsie paused at the pleading in her mother's voice.

"Honey, I am sorry about the fight we had a couple of months ago. I know I should have called to talk to you about it, but I couldn't figure out where to start. I was surprised and embarrassed when you, um, walked in that day. I did not respond well at all. You should have told me about the baby."

Kelsie sighed. "Yeah, well, I was a little preoccupied that day too. I might have told you. But I knew what you would say. What you would all say. And then you told me to get out without so much as noticing that I was upset too."

She heard her mother's intake of breath.

"I thought," her voice cracked. "I thought that maybe if I just took care of myself for a while. Maybe then you wouldn't treat me like I'm helpless. I'm not, you know. Not helpless at all. I have a job and a home and will be graduating and taking the bar exam. And I'm doing it all without your help. But here I am and the first thing you do is accuse me of being helpless."

She looked around the room, at her mother's stricken look and Helmut's scowl. At the way Rob glanced at the door as though he couldn't wait to leave.

"I think," she said slowly. "I think that I've had it wrong all this time. You all keep telling me that I'm the weak one. But you guys are the ones who can't handle your own problems. Helmut gets mad and starts bossing everyone around. Rob just takes off and stops talking to everyone. And you, Mom, decided that the problems are just too hard to solve, so you don't even try. Guess what, everyone, you aren't my problem anymore. I have myself and my baby to worry about, and right now, I don't need all your problems too."

CHAPTER SIXTEEN

Kelsie reached her car door, her vision blurred with hot, angry tears. She fumbled for her keys and swore when she couldn't find them in her purse.

Just like Helmut said. Can't even keep track of my car keys.

She was stronger than that. She would be. After the words she'd flung at her family just now...she had to be. She plunged her hand into the bag again, determined to succeed this time.

"Mind if I drive?" asked Rob from over her shoulder. "I took your keys earlier anyway."

She whirled. "You what?"

"I didn't mean to upset you," he said softly, soothingly. "I took them from the top of your purse right before I gave it to you and offered to drive you home. I really do need the fresh air. Come on, I bet you're starving. Let me find you dinner."

She noticed that he had his backpack slung over one arm. He was prepared to leave the house, too.

He opened the passenger door for her, and waited while she climbed in. It felt awkward sitting on the wrong side of her car.

They drove in silence for a while. Kelsie swiped the rest of her tears off her face and calmed her breathing.

"Do you hate me? Do you think I was wrong to run away?" Rob finally asked.

She squeezed her eyes shut as she tried to corral ten years' worth of emotion into a coherent answer. "No."

"No, you don't hate me or no, you don't think I was wrong?"

"I don't hate you. I miss you. When you left, all I had left was Helmut and Mom. That was right after Helmut's other girlfriend had died in her own car crash, do you remember? Even before you left...he was just mad all the time back then. I didn't understand why. Then you guys started fighting with each other, and you were never around. And then you were just gone."

"I'm sorry. It didn't have anything to do with you."

"I get that, now. But I was twelve when you left. I didn't understand then."

Rob pulled the car into a spot along the main strip and parked. "I was only eighteen. I didn't understand either. I still don't, not really. But I do think I was wrong to run away."

Kelsie nodded. "Me too. But we all make stupid choices sometimes."

"Yeah."

She reached over and grabbed his hand from the steering wheel and gave it a squeeze.

He squeezed back. "I've made plenty of stupid mistakes. I guess it's time to stop running from them. Come on, let's go have dinner."

Kelsie climbed out of the car, but pulled up short when she got to the sidewalk. She was less than a block from Marq's restaurant. "I'm not that hungry."

Rob took her gently by the elbow and steered her towards the door. "Your stomach was growling while we were driving, so I know that's a lie. Besides, you ate a whole tray of brownies from this same restaurant while I was at your apartment last week."

Her heart thudded in her chest as she grasped for any excuse to turn back. "I don't think this is a good idea."

He shot her a hard look then reached for the door. "Time to quit running from problems."

The Christmas Eve crowd was thin and the bakery case nearly empty. Marq's feet ached from spending hours behind the register ringing up trays of cookies and other desserts, and his neck ached from the extra hours he'd spent hovered over the stove filling in for one of the line cooks who hadn't come in. At less than an hour before closing time, the end was in sight. Sofia had mixed up a large pitcher of eggnog to share with the staff after the last customer left. After that, he planned to crash early and sleep late before time to go celebrate with Joaquín tomorrow afternoon.

The bell on the front door announced another customer, and he sighed. Maybe they just wanted a cake. He cast a longing glance at the long stainless steel prep table that he'd just cleaned. Maybe they wouldn't want dinner.

"I think you should take this one, Marq," said Sofia as she peered out across the dining room from the kitchen entrance.

"Why not." He tossed a dirty towel into the bin then washed his hands and ran them through his hair to smooth it back. He tried to fix a smile to his face as he stepped into the dining room.

Only a couple of tables were occupied, one of them by Rob.

His steps faltered and he raised an eyebrow at Sofia. "How did you know who he was?"

She gave him a puzzled look. "I have no idea who that man is. But he is with your *novia*."

Novia. Sweetheart. Girlfriend. *Kelsie*.

Marq's mouth went dry as Rob shifted in his seat, revealing the woman sitting beside him.

She was looking around the room anxiously. Looking for him?

He approached their table cautiously. Kelsie's face froze when he got close.

"Rob, you came." He offered his hand and Rob stood and shook it. "Merry Christmas."

"Merry Christmas. I'm glad you're still here. I wasn't sure if the place would even be open today." Rob glanced around the room. "This is awesome."

Rob motioned toward an empty chair and Marq sat, answering his old friend's questions about the restaurant, and his career. Kelsie kept quiet and studied the menu intensely, like she were memorizing it.

"We are both starving. What do you recommend?"

"Let me take care of the order. It's good to see you again, Kelsie."

That got her attention. She folded the menu and smiled at him, cautiously. Fleetingly. Her cheeks looked rounder than the last time he'd seen her, and her eyes were red like she'd been crying.

"It's good to see you too."

The detachment in her gaze, in her voice, stung. Marq shoved his chair back. "I'll be back. Let me go get your dinner started."

He heard whispered voices between the siblings as he walked away, but couldn't tell what they were saying. He fired off instructions to Sofia and the other line cook, then walked to the bar. He grabbed a beer for Rob, and opened a bottle of wine, one of the reds that Kelsie had loved last summer, and poured two glasses.

She never told her brother.

The knowledge twisted in his heart.

He picked up the two wine glasses in one hand and palmed the beer in his other. High school was a long time ago. Now that the prodigal brother had returned, maybe Kelsie's crazy family would start talking again. Start forgiving each other. They might even forgive him. And he and Kelsie could start this relationship over from the beginning. Do things the right way. Show the family that he had grown up.

Kelsie sat stiff-backed in her seat, clutching her coat to her chest with both hands. Rob was leaning back, glaring at his sister.

Marq glanced between them as he set out drinks. "Everything okay?"

Rob gave him an unreadable look and took a long swig of his beer.

"Let me guess. It's Christmas Eve, and the two of you are sitting in a restaurant instead of home in front of a Christmas tree. Family squabble?"

Kelsie's eyes flickered his way, then away. She didn't touch her drink.

Rob gave his sister a hard look and then nodded down towards Marq's forearms on top of the table. "The ink is new."

Marq forced himself to smile around grit-ted teeth. "Yeah," he said quietly.

"I don't recognize the symbols. Do they mean anything? Or is it just art?

Marq stretched out his right hand. "They mean something. I got this one here," he pointed at a snake that twined from his wrist up to his elbow. "Six months into my stint at Baker Cor-rectional Institute. I was part of the *La Familia* gang for a while. Toughest guys on the cell block. Most of them were in for murder, armed robbery, that kind of thing. They were the first friends I made when I got there. Told me they'd watch my back, since I was so young. Said they'd set me up in business when I got out. Dealing. Good money, they promised."

Rob frowned.

Marq turned his left wrist over, revealing a set of raised scars disguised under a colorful half-sleeve tattoo. "One day, some new toughs had just transferred from Okeechobee. One of them remembered me. We--the two of us--had bought some weed off him a few times. He ac-cused me of snitching to the cops. He jumped me. Had stolen a butter knife from the kitchen. Sharpened it on rocks when no one was watch-ing. Most of the gang, my so-called friends, they just watched. He slashed me a bunch of times, on the arm, on my shoulder, one good gouge on leg."

He stared at the table, forcing back the

memory.

"The guards took their time breaking it up. Only one guy even tried to help me. He got a few cuts too."

"Shit," muttered Rob.

"That was how you met Wei?" asked Kelsie softly.

Marq reluctantly sought her eyes. He wasn't sure what he would see in them. Pity? Disgust? Her face was white, but her eyes were warm. Worried.

She touched his arm, her fingers barely brushing along the scars. Marq shivered.

"Yeah. We decided to look out for each other after that. And to get the hell out of there and stay out."

Rob set his beer bottle down hard enough to jolt Marq's attention away from Kelsie.

"How can you do it?" Rob asked, his voice hard.

"Do what?"

"Sit here with me, make me food and bring me a drink and not just punch my lights out? You smile and ask about my work and my family...the same family who fucked you over. If I were you, I would be back in that kitchen, dumping rat poison in our dinner."

A chill settled over Marq. "It's not like that. Not anymore."

"Like hell it's not."

"Rob." The word was a question on Kelsie's tongue. Or maybe a warning.

Rob looked from Kelsie to Marq and then laughed. Bitterly. "Here I thought I was doing you a favor, little sis. I thought I was going to reunite you with your fling and give you both my blessing, for whatever that was worth. I thought I was here to help you."

Marq's stomach clenched. *Rob knew about Kelsie.*

"But the joke's on me after all. Do you want to know why he hasn't dragged me out to the alley and beat me senseless? After I got him sent to jail? Slashed me with a sharp butter knife like the punks who jumped him? I killed his cousin, you know. Driving drunk. I should have died that night, not Joaquín. I deserved it." Rob pushed himself back from the table.

"Rob?" Kelsie's voice cracked.

"I killed his cousin and left the cousin's unborn baby without a father. I abandoned him to die in prison while I jetted off to college with a clean record. And now he has his revenge."

"It's not like that, Rob. I'm not after revenge. We were kids. We were stupid. I deserved what I got. I don't hate you at all. I swear to God I don't," Marq said quietly. He could see that Rob wasn't buying it.

"Go ahead and stand up, little sister. Show my old friend just how complete his revenge was. Show him your secret."

Marq's mouth went dry as she stood.

Slowly. Still clutching her coat to her chest like it was some kind of goddamned shield. He knew. Damnit, he knew before she dropped the fabric to the ground. Knew from the round of her cheeks. From the shame and pleading in her eyes. Knew before he ever saw the swell of her belly.

Kelsie held her breath as she watched the play of emotions across Marq's face. Watched him pale with shock, then flush with anger. And then shutter.

"We should talk." Her words were barely above a whisper. It was all she could manage.

He shook his head like he was trying to clear it. "Why didn't you tell me?"

She bit her lip, trying to summarize months' worth of agony and shame into something that he could understand. "Our agreement...I didn't think you..."

"Didn't think I what? Could handle it? Could take care of you? Could handle a baby?" His words were flat, cold.

"No! I mean yes. Yes, you could take care of me. But I don't need you to. I don't want--"

He sneered. "It's pretty obvious what you don't want."

Rob placed a hand on her shoulder. "Come on, let's get out of here."

She looked at Marq, opened her mouth to say something. But the words wouldn't come.

He turned away.

Rob gave her arm a light tug, but she pulled away.

"You would make a great father. You're so happy with your nephew, so good with him. You're his father, no matter what the birth certificate says. And I don't want to take that away from him, or from you. I never intended to mess up your little family. To mess up the life that you've built."

Marq didn't answer. Around her, the restaurant was quiet. The door chimed as a few straggling customers left. The hostess out front turned off the lights by the bakery case. The Christmas Eve shift was coming to a close. Kelsie blinked, trying to hold back tears, but they flowed anyway. Stupid, stupid pregnancy hormones.

"I never meant to keep this from you. I just hadn't figured out how to tell you yet."

"And the divorce papers?" he asked quietly.

Rob made a small noise behind her, but she ignored him.

"This is why everything got delayed. If I had never...even if I never got brave enough to face you, you would have found out in court in the spring." She wiped her hand across her eyes. "I'm a coward, okay? I was scared so I ran away.

Call it a family trait."

Rob snorted. She elbowed him in the ribs.

"Look, we don't have to talk about this now."

He turned back, still not meeting her eyes.

"Shall I take you home?" asked Rob quietly.

"Wait," said Marq. "Can I..."

Her breath hitched, waiting for him to finish the question.

He took a step forward. Reached out his hand. "Can I touch the baby?"

She nodded. Took his hand. He stepped in closer. She pressed his palm to one side where she felt a fist-sized lump. Baby butt or head, she wasn't sure.

Marq's hands on her belly were warm, comforting. He moved his hands around, gently feeling the baby bump. Kelsie sucked in her breath and inhaled his scent. He smelled sweet like pancakes and a little bit spicy, with an underlying hint of his soap.

The sound of plates shattering on the kitchen floor broke both of them out of the moment.

Marq turned and frowned.

Julie stood by the swinging door to the kitchen, hands spread wide and a pile of broken porcelain by her feet. "Sorry. They slipped."

"Why are you here tonight, Julie? I thought you and Joaquín had plans." Marq and

Rob exchanged a meaningful glance.

Tension in the room crystalized, sharp and dangerous.

Julie stepped over the broken dishes and walked slowly, calmly to where the three of them stood. Kelsie tensed, remembering the last time Julie had walked in on her and Marq.

"Rob Forrester," the name was soft on Julie's tongue. "I haven't seen you in years."

"Julie Alvarez. You look well," nodded Rob.

She smiled sweetly. "So do you. I just stopped by to say a quick Merry Christmas to Marq and Sofia. It looks like there are a few cookies left in the case. Mind if I take some home with me? I've got people coming over tonight."

Kelsie stood frozen, but Julie just walked past her without even a glance.

It wasn't possible for the other woman to have missed Marq's hands on her pregnant belly. She couldn't reconcile how calm Julie looked while loading cookies from the bakery case into a cardboard box with the broken dishes still by the kitchen door. Or with the screaming harpy she had last seen at the hospital when Joaquín got hurt.

"We should go," Kelsie said.

Marq nodded. "It is closing time."

Julie sauntered back past them toward the rear of the restaurant, her face looking smugly pleased. It gave Kelsie a chill.

"We still need to talk," Marq called softly after them as she and Rob left.

CHAPTER SEVENTEEN

Rob drove her to her apartment and spent the night on the couch. On Christmas morning, after coffee and cold cereal, he took off on foot. He said he needed to clear his head and walking was the best way to do it. And he promised to call her if he needed anything. He didn't. But he did text later in the afternoon to say he had booked a flight back to Rio.

Kelsie napped most of Christmas day, and purposefully ignored the phone messages left by her mom, by Helmut, by Claire. Alice came home with leftovers later in the evening and was disappointed she had missed seeing Rob again. Kelsie tried not to roll her eyes or to point out the fact that Rob had barely glanced at Alice when he was here before.

The day after Christmas, Kelsie and Alice went shopping. For the first time, she allowed herself too look at baby clothes, and bought a few things from the clearance racks. The ranges of baby clothes sizes, from the doll-like preemie to the 36-month ones that fit a larger toddler were confusing. But she found Christmas-y bibs and a blanket and an adorable knit Santa hat for next year.

"Merry Christmas, Mrs. Martin." Kelsie said with a smile as she and Alice climbed the steps towards their apartment, shopping bags slung over their shoulders.

Mrs. Martin shot Kelsie a disapproving look, her lips pursed and hands on hips. Kelsie kept her smile bright as she passed. She was in no mood to feed yet another person's disapproval.

Alice took the stairs two at a time. Kelsie stopped in the middle to catch her breath. She made a point of staying active, walking as much as possible and doing light workouts at the gym like her doctor suggested. But still she huffed.

Alice let out a noise that was halfway between a squeak and a chirp.

"What's the matter?" Kelsie turned the corner of the landing, but couldn't see her friend's feet on the stairs above her at all.

"Nothing," called Alice. "Well, not nothing. But nothing bad. I think. Oh, just hurry up."

"Someday you will be the one with a basketball for a belly and I will be the one telling you to hurry up while you're gasping for breath."

At the top of the stairs, she stopped short.

Marq leaned against the wall next to her

front door. His muscled arms were crossed across his chest, and the deep tan of his biceps stood out in contrast against the white fabric of his T-shirt. Narrow hips and toned thighs strained against a pair of form-fitting black jeans. His short black hair was lightly gelled and combed back out the way of the dark chocolate eyes that burned with a dark intensity.

Her already shaky breath caught in her throat and her belly gave a small flip. For once, she was pretty sure that was NOT the baby kicking. She clutched the railing for a minute to steady herself as stars danced across her vision.

The next thing she knew, Marq's arms were around her shoulders and Alice was fretting with the door. Then they were all inside and she was on the couch with her feet up and two anxious faces peering at her. Marq took her suddenly freezing fingers in his.

"I'm fine. Really."

Marq shook his head. "Your face went white."

"Fainting spells are common during pregnancy," added Alice.

Kelsie and Marq looked at her.

"What? I read your 'What to Expect' book."

Kelsie narrowed her eyes.

Alice rolled hers. "I have some, um, errands to run. See you guys later."

Kelsie snuck a glance at Marq as Alice

gingerly stepped out of the apartment, closing the door behind her. He swept his hand across the faded blue-and-white checked couch. The cushions sagged despite the extra foam she and Alice had added, and the fabric of the arms was discolored from use despite their best efforts with the steam cleaner. But overall it was in good condition. And it had been free, including the matching oak-colored coffee and end tables with their Queen Anne legs and their shiny brass hardware.

"Was this from your mom's house?" he asked.

She nodded.

"If you count all the nights I crashed on this couch....months, probably." A smile ghosted across his features. "Do they know?"

Her family. She shook her head. "They just know that I'm pregnant, not about you. They found out Christmas Eve, just like you did."

He looked away, his mouth a hard line.

"Sit down. On the couch, please, or in a chair. I won't talk to you while you're squatting on the floor."

"Yes, ma'am," he said half under his breath. But he stood up and sat on the armchair across from her. He leaned forward, elbows on his knees. "I want to be involved. I deserve to be involved."

Kelsie's belly roiled. This time it was the baby, flipping over or doing gymnastics or whatever he or she was doing in there. She put a hand to one side of her abdomen and felt the hard lump of a head, or maybe a backside.

"This isn't about your family, Kelsie. I don't know what you want," his voice broke a little. "I don't even know if you want to keep the baby. But this is about *my* family. And you and that baby are mine. For now anyway."

She took a deep breath. She had imagined this moment a hundred different ways. Some involved roses, others storms of tears. Sometimes angry silences and slamming doors. This was different. This was the two of them, alone, sitting on her mother's discarded couch. Raw. Honest. "I am keeping my baby."

"I want to be involved. Everything. Going to the hospital. Setting up the crib. Going to the doctor...." He fixed her belly with a look of wonder. "Is it a girl or a boy?"

Kelsie patted the baby bump, not sure if she were soothing the child or herself. "I don't know. I had an ultrasound, but the doctor couldn't tell. The baby kept its legs crossed."

"You got to see the baby? Did they give you a photo?"

Her face flushed as a wave of emotion passed over her. He looked so excited. So interested. So scared.

"Let me find them." She pushed herself to standing, feeling self-conscious and far from graceful.

Marq followed her to the bedroom and hung in the doorway while she rifled through her dresser drawer. She had gone to the ultrasound before Thanksgiving with Alice. Her friend had chattered happily while the technician squirted KY Jelly on her belly. Alice oohed and aah'ed at the grainy black and white alien on the screen. Kelsie had watched the whole process as though she were only a casual observer. Like it was a TV show instead of her own life. She had already decided, before then, that she was going to keep the baby. But it still hadn't felt real.

Now here was Marq, looking so intense and interested. For the first time in months, she felt a tiny sliver of hope pierce the fog around her heart.

A week later, Marq stood in Kelsie's tiny apartment kitchen and shook his head sadly as he peered through the oven door.

"This," he jabbed a finger at the grimy glass door obscuring the thermometer that hung inside, "Is the sorriest excuse for a cooking appliance I have ever seen. It has been pre-heating for half an hour and is barely over 200 degrees."

"Actually, if you turn it up above 400, then it gets way too hot and burns everything." Kelsie sat perched at the counter wearing a silly decorative apron that barely tied at her waist. The thing was all but useless anyway. It was too flimsy with too many frills. It would never last a day in his restaurant. He would have to bring her a real one.

"How do you cook anything like this?"

Her cheeks colored. "I don't really bake. Mostly warm food up in the microwave. The only thing I ever make in the oven is cookies, and it does 375 just fine."

Marq scanned the groceries he'd set out on the counter, re-thinking his plans. He could switch out the roasted chicken entree he had been planning for a sautéed one instead. And as long as he kept an eye on the oven temperature, he could probably use it for the vegetables. He was determined to make this work.

He had spent several long hours on the phone the past two weeks trying to talk Kelsie into moving back to Palm Beach with him. She refused. She had one last semester of college left. He could respect that. She had worked hard to get this far in law school. He didn't want to be the one to stop her now.

No, he was just the one to knock her up.

He could fix that. He knew he could. The baby wasn't due until after graduation, so school should be no problem. And it was only an hour drive to her place from his. He knew he needed to back off in the restaurant kitchen and let more of his staff run the place. They were capable. He had trained them himself.

Wei kept reminding him that now--while the restaurant was hot and talked about--now was the time to branch out. Think about his next venture. He couldn't do that if he spent every day slaving over the stove or pouring drinks.

The plan was for him to work a mix of days and evenings, always taking 2-3 days every week off. Like a real weekend, except mid-week. On those days, he would drive to Miami and go to doctor appointments with Kelsie. And do other important father-to-be stuff, whatever that was.

After the baby came, he could work his restaurant thing around her lawyer thing. He would find a way.

Tonight, finding a way meant making sure his wife and baby had a delicious home-cooked meal.

"You look so serious. Is dinner totally ruined?" Her eyes looked wide with worry.

He could fix that too.

"Nope. Just mentally rehearsing. Did you know that cooking, when done well, is a performance art?"

She glanced at the groceries and back to him, one eyebrow raised. "Does that mean you're going to start juggling the potatoes?"

He grinned. "I might." He set his tool box on the counter and started to unlatch it.

"Is that a drill?"

Marq laughed at the alarm in Kelsie's voice. "My knives. We chefs always bring our own."

He pulled out his favorite all-purpose chopping knife, gave the edge of the blade a quick check, then took out his sharpening steel and swiped it until the point was just right.

Kelsie had to rifle through three different cupboards before finding him a cutting board. He made a mental note to prepare enough leftovers for a couple of nights' dinners before he went home. Clearly, she and her roommate were incapable of properly feeding themselves.

"I found someone to help with your situation with Sofia," she told him as he was trimming the ends of asparagus spears. "If you still want help, that is."

He paused. "What kind of help?"

"One of my law professors from last year specializes in immigration law. I told her about the situation--not about the stealing--and didn't mention your restaurant. Just the situation in general. She wants to help."

"That is good. I've got good news. Two gallons of milk and about a hundred dollars worth of beef disappeared from the refrigerator overnight earlier this week."

She cringed. "How is that good news?"

"Sofia was out of town all week. Visiting her brother. She isn't the thief." He tossed the asparagus with some olive oil. "Do you think your professor friend can get her a green card? Because her recipe for a cinnamon-chocolate bar just got a rave review in in the Lifestyles section of the Palm Beach Post. And I found out that both of her kids are making honor roll at their high school. I really don't want to lose her."

"Let me get you the professor's phone number."

He talked throughout the rest of ingredient prep work. Talked more about his restaurant, about the food, asked about her classes and professors. He couldn't stop himself from adding a few flourishes to the chopping and slicing and dicing. His pride puffed as she held her breath while he sliced the potatoes into perfect one-eighth inch disks. He pulled all his best tricks, and she watched appreciatively.

"So tell me," he asked once the veggies were safely roasting at exactly 375, "What happens after graduation?"

Her bright grin faded just a shade and she carefully counted out silverware and lined it up on the counter before answering. "First, I have to sit for the bar exam."

"That's like a really big test, right?"

She shrugged. "Yes. I start studying for it this semester. I planned it that way from the beginning. Made sure I had a light load at the end so I could get a jump start. It's a tough job market right now, so I wanted every advantage I could get when I start interviewing."

He removed the whole chicken from its butcher paper wrapping and started carving. He was originally just going to butterfly it, but that would never fit in Kelsie's frying pan. "Do you have any interviews lined up yet?"

Kelsie took a deep breath and paused, with her hand on her belly. "Sorry," she said with a faraway smile. "The baby just kicked me hard in the ribs. Here, do you want to feel it?"

Marq set down the knife and washed his hands as fast as he could. But when she took his hand and placed it on her belly, he felt nothing.

Kelsie frowned and moved their hands. She held him up at the top of the baby bump, so close to her breasts that with one deep breath, his knuckles would brush those sweet curves.

A rush of heat hit him below the belt. Marq took a gentle step back. They had talked a lot lately, all about the pregnancy. And the baby. And not a word about the two of them as a couple.

"She stopped moving when you got close," she said.

Kelsie's cheeks looked fuller than they had last summer. Fuller cheeks, fuller breasts. Her face was flushed from the warmth of the kitchen, or maybe from her giggling. The flush crept down her collar bone to the exposed skin of her neck. It crept down the clingy T-shirt that outlined those breasts.

Marq turned abruptly back toward his

chopping block. And the chicken breasts.

She bustled around him in silence while he finished prepping the rest of the food on the stove top. He wasn't sure why getting out plates and glasses took so much activity, but he was both grateful and annoyed to have the quiet.

"I have to wait until later to start job hunting," Kelsie said finally.

He looked up from the sizzling meat. Her eyes didn't meet his.

"I was going to start sending out resumes this month, but my advisor told me not to. Discriminating against a person because of a medical condition like pregnancy is technically illegal but..."

He closed his eyes for a minute, feeling her disappointment like a sucker punch to the gut. "Yeah. Discriminating against someone for being Latino is technically illegal too. It still happens. It happens even to guys who don't have a rap sheet."

"True. I'm sorry. I have no business complaining, I guess. Especially to you."

He looked up sharply. "I'm the reason you're in this mess. Complain all you like. And I do all right with the restaurant. You can take your time finding a job after the baby gets here. I guarantee you will not starve."

Before he could blink, she was in tears. Gushing, blubbering tears. He moved the chicken off the heat and took her in his arms. She curled against his chest, leaning her head onto his shoulder, and sobbed. He had never seen anyone turn on the water works so fast and so hard. All he could say was "shh".

"Do you promise not to just disappear?" she asked finally between shuddering breaths. "Not that you need to always be here every minute or anything..just..just..just please don't take off and leave me--don't leave the baby--all alone without warning. My father died really quick, you know. One morning he was there at breakfast, and then he just never came home."

Marq stroked her back and waited for her to continue.

"Rob got on a plane one day for Brazil. He didn't tell me he was going. Didn't tell me he wasn't planning to come back for good. And now Helmut..."

"Where did Helmut go?"

"He told me to go take care of myself. I mean, I can take care of myself. But he's my big brother. And he has always been around before. Every time I needed him, he was there. But not now. If you have to go, give me time to get used to it."

He kissed the top of her forehead. "I'm not going anywhere Kelsie. I promise."

Kelsie leaned on Marq's strong shoulders, with her cheek nestled in the crook of his neck. He smelled lovely, like soap and spice. His hands traced lazy circles on her back, and he was warm. So very warm. Heat radiated through their shirts. She felt every small movement, every breath that they took like fire on her sensitive breasts. The bare skin of his neck and ear sat tantalizingly close to her mouth. She longed to kiss it, to taste him.

She should pull away. Nothing was settled with them. Nothing was certain. Living the last few months alone with nothing but the memory of his smile, the memory of his touch, had been hard. She lay awake some nights remembering the glow of his eyes, the way he could make her laugh, the way he could make her melt.

She drew in a ragged breath and shifted her stance. Heat poured through her skin. Her nipples begged to be touch. Her sex throbbed.

The past week had been a whole new brand of torture. Marq called her every night and texted several times a day. She found herself laughing at stories he told, and pouring out details of her days, her schooling, her plans. She caught herself glancing at her phone, waiting for the next message, hoping for it to ring, loving the sound of his voice on the other end.

All week she looked forward to tonight's visit. The first of many, he had promised. She had so many things to show him. Paperwork, notes from the doctor visits, a copy of a child-birth book written just for expectant fathers. Mostly, she wanted his smile. Wanted his company. She was so afraid that something would come up and keep him away.

Now he was in her arms and saying all the right things about family and the future and his hands were on her body.

She wanted those hands everywhere.

Kelsie felt his pulse racing. Saw the flush of his skin. Felt the circles on her back slow as his hands drifted lower, to her waistline.

"Marq?" It was barely a whisper.

He answered with a kiss. Light, tentative, sweet.

She wanted more. She slipped her arms up around his neck and pulled his head down to hers. She was rewarded with a groan as his mouth slanted over hers as he tasted her and she tasted him. His hands swept the curve of her back, pulling her close against him, not close enough.

She ran her fingers through his hair, traced his earlobe and the side of his neck.

His finger ran up the sides of her ribcage, cupped her aching breasts. His thumbs brushed gently over her nipples and she gasped as he repeated the move, harder.

He broke from her mouth and kissed her cheek to her temple and whispered in her ear. "I want you so bad right now."

She grinned and ran her hands down his chest to the hem of his shirt. "Come to bed."

Marq pulled away for a minute and she nearly pouted until she realized he was turning off the stove and the oven and covering up the partially cooked dinner. She took his hand in hers and led him to the bedroom.

She helped pull his shirt off and ran the palms of her hand down his chest to his waistband. He held his breath as she unbuttoned his jeans. His cock was hard and strained at the zipper. She cupped the hard length and was rewarded with a gasp. Then he pulled her hands away.

"Not so fast. You first."

She blushed as he removed her T-shirt. She watched, uncertain what he would think when he saw her naked. The last time they were together, she had been slender and curvy. Now the curves were all in her belly. She didn't have to wait long.

He started kissing at her collar bone, and only barely paused at the swells of her breasts to nibble her lightly through her bra before unfastening that. His hands were everywhere. Around her back, her belly, cupping her breasts, sliding down the back of her leggings and then inside them. Soon he had those off her too and gently walked her back until she sat on the edge of the bed.

And then he knelt. In front of her.

"You are so damned beautiful," he whispered. And then took her clit in his mouth.

He licked and sucked while his fingers parted her damp flesh. Teasing and probing.

Kelsie lay helpless in ecstasy. Her legs were spread wide for him and his tongue was on her and inside her. He lifted her butt, positioning her even more open, his hands tracing the sensitive skin at her anus at the same time his tongue found the hard nub of nerves inside her.

Tension wound in her and she moaned and gasped and thrashed and pleaded.

"More. Harder. Please don't stop."

Then she broke. Her sex tightened around his fingers and the waves shook her. He kept his fingers there as the waves began to subside and dragged his lips from her clit with a gleam in his dark eyes that warmed her to her already molten core.

He shucked his pants and boxers and then joined her, standing between her still open legs at the side of the bed. He bent down and kissed her deeply. She tasted her own salty flavor on his tongue. They kissed until she was throbbing again and she rubbed her damp cleft against the hard length of his shaft. He was heat and friction between her legs and she wanted him inside her.

"Wait," he said. "Do we need a condom?"

"Have you been with anyone since..." She couldn't quite bring herself to finish the question.

He shook his head. "No one since you."

She smiled, relieved. "Then we should both be good to go."

He smiled, a beautiful, feral smile.

She pulled him closer, up and onto the bed where she could reach him. Could reach every inch of his bronzed skin. Could reach the line of black hair that led downward. Could cup his cock and his balls and squeeze and play until he hissed and gasped and lay back with a look of pure pleasure on his face.

She straddled him, enjoying the friction of his legs against the softer skin of hers. She climbed downward until she could take him in her mouth the way he had taken her.

Teasing. Tasting. Licking. Sucking. Her hands worked his length while her tongue worked the tip of his shaft until his breath was ragged.

"Please," he begged.

She was wet and throbbing with anticipation.

She slowly crawled back upwards, letting his cock glide between her breasts and down her abdomen until she straddled his hips.

With one hand between them, she grasped the hard rod and settled him at her opening. Then slowly, oh so slowly, sank onto his shaft. She shuddered with pleasure at his thickness, his heat.

Together they began to move. Gasping, groaning. She rocked her hips and he held them down to help drive deeper. Slower. Then faster.

One of his hands found her clit and teased it while his cock slid into her. The other hand caressed her breasts. Squeezed nipples. She wound up tighter. Higher than last time.

Over and over the waves of pleasure built until she came again. Hard, tight spirals slammed over her and he slammed into her, grasping her hips in both hands to keep their pace as she rode him until he was spiraling with her.

His thrusts slowed as the ripples of her climax slowed until they were both spent and she sagged down.

He gently helped her off of him and she lay, curled in his arms, back to front as their breath slowed.

"Are you hungry?" he asked between light kisses on the nape of her neck.

Kelsie yawned. "Mmm-mm. A little. Sleepy too."

He chuckled. The sound was a low rumble in her ear.

"Marq?" she asked as sleep dragged her down into its sweet darkness.

"Hmm?"

"Don't go yet," she said.

"I'm not leaving."

"Good," she said. Then thought with a

sleepy smile, *I love you*.

CHAPTER EIGHTEEN

When the alarm sounded on Marq's phone, the clock on the table read five A.M. The spring days were beginning to lengthen, but it was still black as night outside.

That wasn't a wake-up call.

Marq sat up in the mostly empty bedroom of his condo and swiped the phone screen. It was the alarm system from the restaurant. It would eventually be wired to call both him and the authorities in case of an emergency, but he hadn't set up the service to start notifying the police yet. The system was still pretty new, and he had no idea if this was the real deal or a false alarm.

The store inventory had continued to come up short some weeks, including during a two-week vacation Sofia took back in February. After that, he started checking the inventory himself, regularly. Stuff disappeared whether Sofia was around or not. It wasn't her. But the pattern didn't match anyone else's work schedule, either.

Finally last week, he had bought a new alarm system. He put it together himself just two nights ago, wandering around the space after closing, climbing ladders to install sensors in the corners, including on the doors to the walk-in refrigerator and freezer units. He programmed it all himself, too, and set it off half a dozen ways just to be sure it worked the way he wanted.

He opened the alarm's app to see what had triggered it. Someone had gone in the back door, the walk-ins, and his office. No one was scheduled to work until nine today.

He swore. Twice.

That was way too many alarms for it to be a programming fault. And today was his day off. He originally was going to drive down to Kelsie's last night after closing, except she had begged him not to. She had an exam first thing in the morning and really needed to study instead of letting him distract her all night.

The way he distracted her most nights he spent down at her place.

He yanked on jeans and grabbed his wallet and cell phone.

Time to find out what was going on for good.

He walked down the back stairs as quietly as he could. There was a van parked in the alleyway, near the kitchen door. He didn't recognize it.

He crept around the side and listened before slowly opening the door and slipping inside. He paused near the employee lockers when he heard voices. At least one man and one woman, heading toward the door. He stepped into the closet alcove where they kept the mops and buckets, behind the half-closed door and watched. Two figures passed through the back door toward the van, their arms filled with boxes of foodstuffs. He couldn't see their faces clearly, but the female figure was too slender to be Sofia.

He bit his tongue to keep from swearing again, then made sure his phone was on silent. He dialed 911.

"I need to report a robbery in progress," he whispered into the phone, keeping an eye on the back door. He ground out the address then quickly ended the call as the back door banged back open. He switched his phone to camera mode.

Only one figure came in this time. A kid. Not just any kid.

Joaquín.

Marq's throat tightened and his gut froze as he watched.

Jo stepped away from the door, his shoulder slumped. The door banged open again and the man walked in and gave Jo a shove. Not enough to knock him down, but not exactly friendly either.

"Go try the safe again, kid. And quit with

your bullshit about not knowing the combination. It's probably your birthday."

Joaquín glared back. "I told you, José, I don't know it."

Marq's jaw clenched as he recognized the man, José. He was the same drug-dealing former employee he'd kicked out of the restaurant on the day he met Kelsie last summer.

José took a swing at Joaquín and landed a punch on his temple. Marq's fists balled and he stepped out of the closet.

"You picked the wrong restaurant to rob and the wrong kid to hit," he growled at José.

The other man took a step back and Marq continued forward, his elbow back and his fist raised.

"Tío, wait. Look be--"

Marq didn't see who hit him with a heavy metal frying pan from behind.

CHAPTER NINETEEN

Kelsie tapped her foot and checked her phone again. Marq was late, and he still hadn't called back. She propped a magazine on top of her bulging lap and tried to flip through the pages. She couldn't concentrate on any of the words. She wasn't even sure which magazine it was. Something with lots of baby pictures inside. She tossed it back onto the waiting room table and crossed her legs.

Her OB was running late and she had been sitting in the waiting room for the better part of an hour and now she had to pee. And Marq was still not there.

Anxiety clawed at the pit of her stomach and the baby gave a hard kick to her bladder. Tears welled up behind her eyes and she pushed herself to standing, feeling about as graceful as a beached whale.

"Excuse me," she asked the receptionist. "Can I use the ladies' room? I don't think I can hold it much more."

The woman at the desk gave her an assessing look over the tops of her reading glasses. She smiled sympathetically. "Sure. But wait just one minute and I will check to see if we need a sample first."

Kelsie nodded and shifted from foot to foot while the receptionist called one of the nurses.

"Go on back. They set a cup in the restroom for you and then go into exam room three when you are done. I'm sorry that you have had to wait so long. By the time I got that far along with all of mine, I felt like I spent half my day waddling to and from the restroom."

Kelsie smiled gratefully. "And if my, er, my husband arrives, can you tell him where I went? He is supposed to be here."

"Of course, honey."

By the time Kelsie had been weighed and prodded, her belly measured, and the baby's heartbeat found, she still hadn't heard from Marq.

Her feet felt like lead as she trudged through the office building to the ground floor entrance. She dialed Alice's cell phone, but it went straight to voicemail. "Hi Alice, it's Kelsie. If you haven't already left town, can you call me back? Marq was supposed to meet me at the OB's office, but he never showed. I need a ride home."

She clicked off the phone, annoyed at herself for not having rented a car. Hers needed some big scheduled maintenance, and the cost of the rental seemed silly when she could ride with Alice to school and then would have Marq around for a couple of days. Alice was headed up to Atlanta for spring break, so Kelsie and Marq would have the apartment to themselves. Alice had dropped her off at the doctor's office earlier, but she was sure that Marq would meet her there for the appointment. He had promised, and hadn't missed one yet.

She glanced up and down the street, then opened the traffic app on her phone and scrolled around on the map, examining his normal route down I95. There were a couple of slow spots on the map, but no accidents. It was the middle of the day, so no rush hour traffic. She sent him one more text message then went back inside the medical building lobby and found a bench.

The knot in her belly wound tighter as she looked up his restaurant's phone number and dialed it.

She never called Marq at work. It wasn't that they were still hiding the relationship. Not exactly. But with Julie's reaction back in the hospital and dropping the dishes at Christmas, Kelsie wasn't eager to wave this in her face. Marq assured her that he was just friends with Julie and that they had never been romantically involved. She believed him. But Marq usually came here to Miami. And he was home in Palm

Beach every weekend.

She held her breath as the phone rang and rang until someone finally answered.

"Hello," said the voice on the other end.

Kelsie puffed out her breath, annoyed. "Um, sorry. I think I have the wrong number. I was trying to call a restaurant."

"Wait, wait. Sorry. Yes, this is Chocolate, Chocolate." The Spanish pronunciation of the restaurant name rolled off the man's tongue.

Kelsie loved the way it sounded in Spanish way better than in English. Cho-co-lah-tay, Cho-co-lah-tay. There were a few waiters who worked there with a similar accent, but she couldn't tell them apart over the phone. "Um, is Marquez Castillo available?"

"No. He is not here right now."

"Ok, can I leave a message for him?"

The man seemed to hesitate. "I can take a message, but I don't know when he will get it. The restaurant is closed today for a, well, for a family emergency."

Just then, the baby kicked Kelsie hard in the ribs and she gasped for breath. Her mind raced with possibilities for what kind of family emergency could keep his precious restaurant from opening, especially on his day off when he wasn't even supposed to be there. It didn't make sense. "Okay. If he comes in, can you have him call Kelsie Forrester?"

"Sure, let me write down your phone

number."

Kelsie rattled off the digits and then slumped against the back of the bench, as much as one could slump while seven months pregnant. She checked her phone again. Alice had texted back. She was halfway to Orlando already--hours away.

She was stranded.

It was actually funny. Getting herself stranded by a guy was how she got herself into this mess in the first place. If she hadn't dumped that cheating volleyball player without waiting for a ride home first, she would never have crossed paths with Marq again. She laughed out loud and put her hand to her bulging belly.

The receptionist behind a desk across the room gave her a funny look, but Kelsie didn't care.

This time, she wasn't helpless. She had a phone with plenty of battery, a credit card, and a pair of comfortable shoes. She could call herself a cab and be home before too long.

Her phone rang, and she recognized the restaurant's phone number. She answered it quickly.

"Kelsie? Marq's *novia*?" asked the woman's voice on the other end.

Kelsie's heart sank a bit when she realized that it wasn't Marq.

"Yes, I'm Kelsie."

"*Dios mío*. Thank goodness you called. I

didn't have your phone number anywhere. I am Sofia. I make the desserts," the words tumbled fast out of Kelsie's phone.

Sofia, not Julie. That was a small relief at least.

But the temporary relief evaporated as Sofia poured out the saga of this morning's events in rapid-fire English that was only occasionally broken by Sofia grasping for the right word. Marq had interrupted a robbery. Kelsie cried out when she heard that Marq had been hurt.

"Do you know which hospital Marq is in?" she asked Sofia.

"*Sí*. But that isn't the worst of it. It's Joaquín."

"Was he there too? Did he get hurt?" Kelsie cringed, knowing that Marq would be sick with worry if something else happened to the boy.

Sofia was quiet for a minute. "No, *señorita*. Joaquín isn't hurt. He is in jail."

Kelsie listened, open mouthed, as Sofia told her the rest of the story. The police had arrived to find Marq unconscious and Joaquín still on the premises. They arrested him and took him to a juvenile detention center. Marq's camera had caught the faces of two other people at the scene--his mother, Julie, and a disgruntled former restaurant employee named José.

"Marq needs you with him," Sofia said. "He is going to need your help. And so is little

Joaquín."

Kelsie closed her eyes. "It will take me a while to get there. I, um, am kind of stuck in Miami at the moment."

This time it was Sofia's turn to listen while Kelsie unloaded the crazy story of the car and how she was stranded.

"Don't you worry," said Sofia at last. "My brother lives not too far away from you. He will pick you up and drive you up to me and I will get you to Marq."

"That is really nice of you, but it's a long drive. I can rent a car. I'm sure I can be there tonight or tomorrow sometime."

"I insist," said Sofia. "It is the least I can do. Marq is like family to me, and I know that you are more than just Marq's girlfriend. That makes you *familia* also. Besides, my brother drives for a limousine service. He is a very good driver."

Kelsie's heart warmed at the word *familia*. Family.

"That would be wonderful, Sofia, thank you."

When she hung up the call a few minutes later, after exchanging more numbers and addresses, Kelsie sat back on her bench. The baby had calmed down its gymnastics routine in her belly. She placed one hand on the side where she could feel the baby pressed against her.

"No matter what happens, baby, I will

always be your *familia*. I promise," she whispered.

CHAPTER TWENTY

Despite the luxury of the rental limousine, the ride from Miami to Palm Beach was horrible. Kelsie's stomach roiled and she had to ask Hugo, Sofia's brother, twice to pull over so she could retch in a ditch along the side of the road. After that, she rode in the front seat, hoping to keep the nausea at bay. She had read in one of her mom-to-be books that it was common for women in their last trimester to have a second wave of morning sickness. The knowledge didn't make her stomach feel any better.

She and Hugo made pleasant conversation for the rest of the drive. He tried hard to keep things light and entertain her with funny stories about his nieces and nephews--Sofia's children. Kelsie insisted that they stop for Sofia before they went to the hospital, and he treated both ladies like celebrities dropping them off at the front door and insisting on opening doors for them.

Hugo was short, round, and bald beneath

his chauffeur's hat with an ample gray mustache over a broad smile. He had the same warm crinkle to his eyes that Sofia always had. Kelsie gave the man a hug in thanks, and he blushed beneath his sun-bronzed skin and tipped his hat.

Sofia took Kelsie's hand and gave it a squeeze. "Let's go find your *novio*, shall we?"

Kelsie swallowed the lump in her throat and walked across the hospital lobby to the information desk. The space was calm and cheery with tasteful flower arrangements and chairs placed in cozy groupings. The serenity of it was totally at odds with her own turmoil of emotions.

"I'm looking for Marq Castillo," she told the gentleman behind the desk. "He was brought in early this morning."

The receptionist scowled slightly as he punched keys on the keyboard. "I am sorry," he said after a minute. "I can only release patient information to immediate family."

Before Kelsie could open her mouth, Sofia stepped forward. "She is his immediate *familia*. See," she pointed to Kelsie's baby bump. "He is her baby daddy."

The man shook his head with a polite, but thin-lipped expression on his face. "I am sorry. Even if I could release information to a fetus, minors are not allowed unaccompanied."

"But, but..." Sofia was getting louder, attracting a few stares from others in the lobby.

Kelsie felt her cheeks redden. She laid a hand on Sofia's arm and tried to draw her back. "It's okay, Sofia"

Sofia opened her mouth to protest one more time and Kelsie shook her head. She turned back to the receptionist and pulled her wallet out of her purse.

"Forgive my friend. We were hoping to keep this a surprise, but that doesn't really matter anymore. Marq is not just my baby daddy. He is my husband."

She tried hard to ignore the gasp of "*Dios mío*," from Sofia. Instead, Kelsie pulled out the copy of her marriage license, her driver's license, and the insurance card that had recently arrived. Marq had been sure to add her to his plan once he realized how expensive all of the doctor visits could be with just Kelsie's bare bones student insurance.

The man behind the desk scowled some more as he punched more keys and then printed a name tag for Kelsie and one for Sofia.

Sofia was still shaking her head when they stepped out of the elevator and found Marq's room. She stayed back while Kelsie lightly knocked on the partly open door and stepped inside.

Marq sat on the side of his bed, with his head in his hands and his elbows on his knees. Underneath an open-backed hospital gown, he wore a pair of scrub-type pajama pants, and an

IV dangled from one arm.

"Hi," she said quietly.

He looked up and their gazes met. His eyes looked tired and drawn, but they lit up at the sight of her. "Hey."

She inched inside the door and closed it lightly behind her. "Sofia told me where to find you. She helped me get here to find you."

A shadow crossed his eyes. "I missed the doctor visit."

She nodded. "How are you? All we know is that you got hit on the head."

He shrugged. "I have a hard head. I will survive. Come here, will you? I can't go very far with all these tubes attached."

She closed the space between him and they melted into each other. He wrapped his hand possessively around her hips and buried his face in her neck. Kelsie shivered as she gently ran her fingers through his hair. "I was so worried about you. When you didn't show up. Then you didn't answer your phone...and then Alice was already out of town..."

He said something then, but the sound was muffled by her hair. Marq took her gently by the shoulders and held her back so that their gazes were even. "Kelsie, I promise you. I would never, ever leave you stranded on purpose. I love you and it kills me to know you were left somewhere alone because of me. I was unconscious half of the morning, and then the hospital phone service wouldn't let me make a long distance call. The cops took my cell as evidence."

Her heart skipped a beat. *Did he really just say...?* Her lips quirked. "From the sound of things, someone could have actually killed you. Now what really happened?"

He patted the visitor chair and she sat as he seemed to gather his thoughts before speaking. The story of the early morning alarm, the burglary, and the assault all came together in fits and starts. In the parts where Kelsie herself would have been sobbing, Marq seemed to draw into himself. To withdraw a little. She took his hands in his.

She could imagine the betrayal he must be feeling. The hurt at having Julie turn on him the way she had.

"Where is Joaquín?"

There, finally, Marq's voice broke. "Arrested."

Kelsie's heart broke for Joaquín...and for Marq. For the teenage Marq she had known, with his life in front of him, about to be decimated. For the Marq who entered prison a boy and left a stronger man. For the one who made a life for himself, and his nephew, despite every roadblock in front of him. And for the Marq who would be a father--was already a father to Joaquín. The pain he was feeling at having his beloved nephew thrown on the same twisted path that he had survived was carved onto his face and into her own heart.

"We will fix it. We will bring him home."

Marq shook his head. "You don't know what it's like for a kid like him. And after the fight at school...no judge will go easy on him."

"Look at me, Marq. I know you had it bad. I do. And I know how awful my family was to you back then. How unfair it was. But it will be different for Joaquín. He has a family. Together we can help him."

"How?" The word was an accusation. "By asking your brothers for help? Do you really think they would help him if they wouldn't help me?"

She kissed him on the forehead. "I wasn't talking about my family. I was talking about you. You and me. We are Joaquín's family, and we will fight for him. Together."

CHAPTER TWENTY-ONE

The next few days were a blur of appointments and meetings. Too many of them were held in police stations and jails. It set Marq's teeth on edge every time he walked into a room full of uniformed officers. His whole life out of prison had been lived on the right side of the law, but he didn't have to like the reminders of his youth and his failures.

Kelsie held his hand through every appointment, and introduced herself as his wife. She looked beautiful, glowing, perfect. She was clear spoken and friendly and communicated well with the police and the lawyers and the representative from the division of family services. She quickly earned a respect from them that Marq never would have had on his own.

She spent hours on the phone with her lawyer friends, and got a referral for one who specialized in both juvenile crime and child custody. Joaquín had to stay in a juvenile center while he waited for a meeting with a judge.

Both the police and the court-assigned counselors who talked to him noted that he had been physically abused by José, Julie's boyfriend. Possibly by Julie herself, which made Marq physically sick. The adults had forced Joaquín to come along for the break-in. The camera footage captured on Marq's cell phone was proof of the abuse and of Joaquín's reluctance.

Their lawyer assured them that they had a good chance of both acquitting Joaquín and getting full custody of him. Julie didn't have any other close relatives, so Marq was Joaquín's closest family. Yes, Marq's prior record could be a problem, but now that he was married and expecting a baby as well as a successful business man, things looked very positive.

There was a small voice in his head that told Marq that Kelsie still planned to leave him. Their marriage wasn't at all as permanent or stable as they pretended for the court. He told the voice to shut up as often as possible.

The police returned Marq's cell phone that next weekend, just in time for Marq to drive Kelsie back to her apartment. She had stayed most of a week and made excuses for her classes. The professors were very supportive, especially since her time spent in courtrooms amounted to extra credit. But finals were looming.

He drove home alone and wandered into his restaurant for the first time since the incident.

Sophia had quietly and competently organized the staff and got the doors back open. Business as usual had never looked so strange to him before. The books didn't need keeping and the kitchen was in good hands. He slinked into his office and shut the door behind him, unable to face the questioning looks and whispered comments.

He dialed Wei.

"Do you need me to come?" his friend asked after hearing Marq's tale. "Say the word and I will be on the next flight out."

Marq smiled to himself. "No, I don't think that's necessary. But I'm glad to hear the words, just the same."

"Any time."

Marq picked up a picture frame from his desk. Joaquín's last school picture. He turned it over and over with his fingers while he talked. "There is something I need help with. It's about Kelsie. I love her."

There was a pause on the other end. "Well, buddy, you know I don't know the girl that well. And I haven't exactly had the best luck with women."

"Oh yeah?" asked Marq. "What about that showgirl you were telling me about over New Years?"

"Long story short," answered Wei. "I don't think I'm the right kind of guy for her."

"Not the right guy for her. But is she the

right girl for you?"

Another pause. "Yeah. She could be. But I screwed up so bad, I don't think I can fix it. Look, if you're asking for my advice, it's simple. Tell her how you feel. Tell her you love her. Tell her every day. And do whatever she needs to feel happy. Take her out on dates to those stupid girly places that women love, buy her flowers, hold her hand. Talk to her. Listen to her. Do stuff with her. Do stuff for her. If it makes her smile at you, do that. Just keep doing that."

Marq leaned back in his chair and put his feet up on his desk. He could hear the half choked sound in his best friend's voice. Could picture the guy's clenched fist and tight jaw as he talked. Man, Wei was deep in love with that showgirl and sounded totally lost. Kind of like Marq himself, actually.

"Just keep doing that," repeated Wei, a little softer.

"I will," said Marq. "Hey Wei."

"Yeah?"

"Why didn't that advice work for you?"

"I told you, buddy. She's too good for me. I let her go. Didn't take any of my own advice. It was better that way. For her."

Marq contemplated the picture frame again. "Thanks, Wei."

"No problem. Let me know when the baby arrives. And good luck."

"You, too."

CHAPTER TWENTY-TWO

Kelsie held Marq's hand while the family court judge delivered her stipulations for Marq and Kelsie's custody of Joaquín. It was temporary, as Julie was still waiting on her own trial to begin. She was seeing a therapist provided by the state and intended to use her current unstable mental state as part of her defense. Julie sent a written letter to the family court judge to that effect, even admitting that she was not currently a fit parent for her son. She pleaded with the judge to let the boy stay with Marq, and sang his praises as a father figure for his nephew.

Kelsie and Marq would have regular checkups with a family therapist of their own, as would Joaquín. The kid had a lot to deal with. Marq fully agreed and their attorney made sure to note that his restaurant insurance policy covered mental health visits.

The judge did suggest, kindly, that the young couple consider their housing arrangements. While the division of family services had judged Marq's apartment to be clean and well cared for, they did point out that with a new baby and a teenager, that the space would soon become cramped.

That was true enough. They had finally moved Kelsie's few belongings in just this weekend after her last final exam, and set up the crib in the condo's one bedroom next to Marq's king sized bed. Marq and his friends had set up a bed in the upstairs loft area for Joaquín. It was accessible by a spiral staircase and while it didn't have real walls, was still enough privacy for now. They could start house-hunting after Kelsie found a job. It would do.

Then the judge was banging her gavel and Joaquín was flying across the courtroom into Marq's arms and both of them were hugging and trying to pretend they weren't crying.

Kelsie sat down and gritted her teeth as another cramp seized her belly. It was her third or fourth during the last hour. She had a few earlier in the morning as well when they were getting ready to go.

She hadn't told Marq. She was afraid he would insist on driving her to the doctor and miss the trial. This was way too important. And the contractions were still really far apart. Nothing to worry about.

"Tía Kelsie. Are you okay?"

Kelsie looked up at Jo, surprised to hear

the title on his lips. *Tía*. Aunt. "I am fine. Just had to sit down."

A wide grin split his face and his eyes lit up and he flung his arms around her neck. "Did Tío tell you we were getting a Wii? You ready for a rematch on that racing game?"

She laughed and tussled his hair. "Any time you want."

Marq took her by both hands and helped her to her feet. He pulled her close for a hug and whispered in her ear. "In case I haven't told you enough the last couple of weeks, thank you for standing by me through all of this."

She smiled. He hadn't just told her how much he loved her. He had brought her brownies and made pancakes, sent her flowers, rubbed her swollen feet and massaged her sore back. And he had made love to her. Slowly, carefully, spooning her while he brought her to blissful completion. It was a position she had come to adore, not just because her pregnant belly was not in the way, but because it left both of his hands free to explore the rest of her body.

Warmth pooled through her at his words. "I promised that I would not give up on you. We are family."

He pulled back and looked into her eyes. "I love you, Kelsie. If we weren't already married, I would be down on one knee right now proposing. The right way. But since we are a little late for that, I want to give you this."

She took the small square box from Marq's hand. Joaquín stood beside him, a cheesy broad grin on his face that made Kelsie think that they had planned it together. Inside the box was a diamond ring. Not big, not expensive, nothing that would ever rival the one that her brother Helmut had given to Claire. It was perfect. "It is beautiful."

"Let me." He took the ring out of the box and tried to slip it onto her left hand. It only made it halfway to the knuckle before it got stuck.

"My fingers have been a little swollen lately," she said, color rising on her cheeks.

Marq brought her fingers to his lips and kissed them. "I thought that might happen."

He opened the bottom of the ring box and pulled out one last surprise. A gold chain to match the gold band of the ring. He took the diamond ring and slipped it onto the chain and then fastened it around her neck.

There was only one thing left to say, but as she opened her mouth to say the words, Marq kissed her. Sweetly, warmly. When he drew back she was breathless.

And then another contraction took hold of her, causing her to gasp. She clutched his hand and tried to breathe deeply, like they had told them in childbirth class.

"Are you okay?" Marq asked, rubbing her back.

She couldn't quite answer at first as the contraction slowly eased. And then she felt the gush of liquid running down her leg. "My water just broke."

CHAPTER TWENTY-THREE

The books all said that labor usually went slow with a first baby. The books were wrong. By the time Marq and Joaquín got Kelsie to his car, the contractions were coming hard and fast. She paid no attention to traffic as he zipped around cars on his way to the hospital. She was only vaguely aware of Marq handing a shell shocked Joaquín his phone and telling him to call Sofia.

The race into the hospital was like a scene from a movie, with Joaquín running ahead yelling that his *tía* was having a baby, and Kelsie panting hard against the waves of contractions, snapping at the nurses who asked her question after infuriating question.

She was deemed ready to push the moment she hit the exam room and less than thirty minutes later, she and Marq had a tiny, purple, squalling lump of a daughter.

Tears of joy and exhaustion and pain

streaked down Kelsie's face as they placed the bundle into her arms for the first time. Once all the messy business was cleaned up, Marq left her side just long enough to go bring Joaquín in from the lobby to meet his new cousin.

"I think you should name her Peach," the boy said.

Kelsie looked down at the slightly lopsided looking head. "Why Peach?"

"She's the princess that Mario and Luigi are always rescuing," he said with a grin.

They all laughed and Marq hugged Joaquín around the shoulders. "You're an awesome kid, did you know that?"

Jo just shrugged.

There was a knock at the door and Sofia poked her head into the room. "Are you up for visitors?"

Kelsie waved her in. "Of course. Come meet our little princess"

Sofia looked hesitant. "I brought some people with me."

The door opened wider and behind her stood Edna and Willard. Kelsie's stomach clenched and tears welled in her eyes. "Mom!"

Her mother was at Kelsie's side in an instant, crying and kissing her daughter. And then oohing and aahing over the new grandbaby.

"I would have called, but there wasn't much time," said Kelsie.

"I came as soon as Sofia called me. You

delivered so fast. I am sorry I missed it. I am sorry that I missed so many things these past few years." Edna pressed her forehead to Kelsie's. "I want to make it up to you. Can you forgive me? Can we start this over again?"

Tears slid down Kelsie's cheeks and her chest felt like bursting with raw emotion. "There has been so much. But first, let me introduce you to someone you used to know. Mom, this is Marq. My husband. And his nephew Joaquín who will be living with us for now. Marq and Joaquín's father were good friends of Rob's back in high school."

Edna straightened and Willard came up to lay a gentle hand on her back. Kelsie looked back and forth between her mother and her husband.

"I remember you Marq. How do you do?" Edna held out a stiff hand and Marq took it.

It was a start. "Mom, I would like to rebuild my relationship with you. But there are rules. First of all, Marq is my family now. My closest family. I love him dearly and he loves me. If you want a relationship with me, it is going to include him. And that is final."

Edna nodded. "I understand. Now may I please hold my granddaughter?"

Kelsie handed over the baby and watched as her mother gazed lovingly at the tiny thing.

"She looks just like you did when you were first born," Edna said after planting a kiss on one tiny cheek.

"I don't know how you can tell. There is more blanket there than baby." Helmut's voice boomed across the already crowded room.

Kelsie saw Marq stiffen and took his hand. "Hello, Helmut. I wasn't expecting to see you."

Her big brother came in carrying a teddy bear and a bunch of foil balloons. He set them down near the foot of her hospital bed and nodded toward Marq.

"I hope I am not intruding. I was at Mom's when she got the call. When your friend Sofia found out which brother I was, she read me the riot act the whole way up the elevator." Helmut nodded back towards where Sofia still waited by the door.

Marq didn't say anything.

"Look, I have done some pretty stupid things in my life," started Helmut.

Marq just waited. Kelsie looked back and forth between the two men. One, the big brother she had always adored. The other, the husband she loved.

"But the stupidest thing I've ever done, by far, was to ignore Kelsie. Without her advice, Claire might never have forgiven me and agreed to be my wife. But more than that. She is my baby sister. I have always protected her, looked out for her. Until you came along."

Marq stood up slowly, despite Kelsie tugging his hand. The room grew quiet as the two men stared eye to eye at each other. "Thank you for looking out for your sister. But you don't need to do that anymore. She has me now. I don't ever intend to let her down"

Joaquín jumped to his feet. "And she has me."

"Yes, she does," said Helmut quietly. "And since I was a total ass at Christmas, I understand if she won't talk to me anymore. I know all about you, Marq. I know your past. And I know what you did for Rob all those years ago. I was an even bigger ass to you than I was to Kelsie. I doubt saying 'sorry' will be enough, but that is all I have. I am sorry."

Marq nodded curtly.

"And thank you. For everything you have done for my family."

"They are my family, too," said Marq.

The room quieted until a nurse tried to come in. "The lactation consultant is here. Oh, my, there are a lot of people."

The baby began to fuss. Kelsie shifted her weight in the bed and felt the painful reminders of her afternoon's exertions. "All right, everyone out. Marq, why don't you take Joaquín to the cafeteria to get him some dinner? And please give me back my daughter."

A few hours later, Marq and Kelsie finally had a few quiet minutes to themselves. The baby slept in a tiny plastic bassinet next to the hospital bed, and Joaquín had left with Sofia. She had promised take him by Marq's apartment first and help him unpack his stuff in his new room, then to her home to hang out for the evening with her own sons. Everyone else had gone home for the night.

Marq lay in the narrow hospital bed carefully cradling Kelsie while she drowsed against his chest.

"I need to tell you something," she said.

"More ice chips?" he asked, already leaning back towards the cup the nurses had left.

"No," she said with a small laugh. "Nothing like that. I have a secret to share."

He kissed her on the earlobe. "Is it a naughty one?"

She elbowed him in the ribs. "With the way I'm feeling right now? No. You heard the nurse. It's going to be a couple of months before we get back to naughty secrets."

He sighed exaggeratedly. "I was afraid of that."

"Then again, my secret is a little naughty."

He growled. "Do I get to hear it or not?"

"Yes. It's about you. Do you know when I the first time I fell in love with you was?"

She felt his body stiffen behind hers.

"I fell in love with you when I was twelve years old. You made me chocolate chip pancakes and made me laugh. And the second time I fell in love with you was when I got hurt in front of your restaurant and you gave me chocolate and shoes. Do you want to know the third?"

"Does it involve more chocolate?"

"No. Do you still want to hear it?"

"Yes." The word was an almost strangled whisper against her ear.

"That is the naughty part. I think it was the night our little princess was conceived in Las Vegas. Do you remember what we did?"

"Yes." This time it was still breathless, but deeper.

She smiled and settled in further, feeling his heartbeat against her ear, seeing the tattoos circling his arms as his arms circled hers. "But I am not done falling in love yet. I hope I am never done. I love you Marq, tonight more than yesterday. Yesterday more than the day before. Now more than last fall."

"I promise," he said. "That you will never have to be done falling in love. Because I never want to be done falling in love with you."

The End

Also by Kristi Lea:

Affairs of the Heart
  The Paris Affair, Volume 1
  The Christmas Affair, Volume 1.5
  The Vegas Affair, Volume 2

Accomplice

Call the Rain